Clarity Bloom

KILLER

RAPIDS

A Clarity Bloom Humorous Mystery Novel

Book 2

MARTINA DALTON

Write as Rain Books

Book Formatting Template by Derek Murphy @Creativindie
Killer Rapids : A Clarity Bloom Humorous Mystery
Copyright © 2020 by Martina Dalton.

For information contact :
Martina Dalton
http://www.martinadalton.com

Book and Cover design by Martina Dalton
ISBN: 978-1-7331168-4-8

First Edition: June 2020

DEDICATION

This book is dedicated to our good dog, Comet, who we were blessed to have as a furry family member for only seven years. We miss you, buddy.

CHAPTER 1

THE SUN BEAT DOWN ON MY BACK as I wheeled the handcart through my Seattle suburb. Even though it was only mid-morning, the heat was getting to me.

The wheels hit a bump in the concrete, and I lurched to the side, nearly hitting the façade of the building before Brandi grabbed me, preventing me from denting the wall.

"Got ya!" Brandi steadied the dolly and straightened the tower of stacked boxes.

I regained my balance and wiped the sweat from my brow. "Thanks. Ten down, one to go." I wheeled the dolly past an outdoor bench and took a hard left through the front door of our new office.

Brandi followed with her hands on her hips. "Tell me one more time why you insist on wheeling that cart with all your stuff from your house to the office?"

I pushed a box off the dolly and opened it. "Because my house is only two blocks away, and because it's good exercise."

Brandi's dark curls bounced as she shook her head. "You're nuts. You almost fell. And it took you an hour to get all this here. You could've loaded your car and driven it here in a few seconds."

I arched an eyebrow. "I sold my roomy BMW, remember? My Prius can't hold eleven good-sized boxes."

"Oh, that's right. I forgot. It would've taken two whole trips." Brandi faked a horrified look. "Well, anyway, I think you could've saved a lot of time by driving."

I wanted to say something in return, but I figured it was pointless to argue. If the three of us were going to get along in a small office, we'd better learn to let some things go.

Jonah opened the door and surveyed the chaos of our unorganized space. "God, this looks awful. Where did all these boxes come from?"

I raised my hand. "They're mostly mine. But it's not just my stuff. It's for the office. I picked up some shelving, a few dishes for the kitchen, and some fun decorative items."

Jonah set down the only box of his stuff on the messy floor. "What about furniture?"

"You mean like desks, tables, and chairs?" I shoved a box toward the wall with my foot.

"Yes. We need to make this place more habitable." Jonah frowned as he glanced around the room.

"Everything will be delivered this afternoon," I said.

"Good." Jonah picked up a box and set it against the longest wall. "But we won't be able to get anything set up if we don't get these boxes out of the way."

As we tried organizing the mess, I thought how different our new life would be after the company we'd worked for had dissolved. Opulent had been an incredible place to work—except when our boss, Paul, had killed my coworker and best friend, Janice. Once Janice had been murdered, everything had gone bad. And then, when the killer had kidnapped my cat and took my parents hostage, life had gone from bad to worse.

2

I still couldn't figure out how we'd worked for a serial killer without knowing it. I shuddered at the memory of Paul trying to drag me into the woods so he could kill me too.

Thank goodness I'd taken a self-defense course from my brother's detective partner, Hunter. The knowledge of how to defend myself had literally saved my life and the lives of my parents and cat, Pumpkin.

"Are you sad you're not working in a swanky office building in downtown Seattle anymore?" Brandi asked Jonah.

"Heck no." He pointed to his casual shirt and cargo shorts. "Now I can wear whatever I want and make my own schedule. And no more sucking up to management."

I laughed. "Now you'll only have to suck up to your clients."

Jonah was a super talented designer. He was what some in the design industry called a "unicorn." That was someone who could do multiple facets of design—web design, visual design, and UX and UI design. He was even a great illustrator. I wasn't sure what all that stuff meant, but I understood it was rare to be good at all of them.

"Don't you worry." Jonah grinned. "I don't mind sucking up to my own clients. They will be well taken care of."

"Speaking of design." I shoved the last box into the row against the wall. "I hope you like the style of furniture I ordered. I should've run it past you both, but it was on sale. I had to decide quickly, since the sale was just for one day."

Brandi shrugged. "We trust you. You have good taste."

"Thanks." I wiped the moisture off my brow. "Anyone need a coffee break? I could use an iced latte."

"I'm in." Brandi grabbed her purse.

"Me too." Jonah held the door open. "After you."

The sweltering heat hit me square in the face when we stepped out onto the sidewalk.

"Oh, it's a scorcher out here." I lifted my shirt away from my skin, hoping the air would dry the moisture.

It was the last week of August, and summer was beating us into submission. But we Seattleites knew that once the relentless rain of late fall settled into the area, we'd be remembering the heat of the summer with fondness.

The Wallingford neighborhood was a quaint area of Seattle, with little shops, flowering baskets, and double-income couples and families. The coffee shop was conveniently located just two stores away from us.

We walked past a man with his Golden Doodle on a leash and a woman pushing a stroller.

The eclectic shops were nestled in neat rows on both sides of the street. I looked back at our office space. It wasn't much to look at on the outside, but it was ours for three years—unless we broke the lease. I hoped our businesses would be successful enough to make it for at least that amount of time.

"What are you calling your CPA business, Brandi?" I opened the door to Lotsa Lattes and ushered my friends inside.

"I gave it a boring, but professional-sounding name. B. Taylor Accounting."

"That works."

We got in line.

"What about you, Jonah?"

He frowned. "I had a hard time deciding, but I had to come up with something for my business license. I'm using my last name. So, it'll be Faulkner Design. And you?"

I'd given the name of my new company a lot of thought. It had to be perfect. Once you nailed down the logo and the branding, it was a real pain to change. Not to mention that if you had to change it, you'd lose any brand recognition you'd earned with your previous branding.

"Bloom Marketing and Investigations. It's quite a mouthful, though."

"Yeah," Jonah said. "It's kind of confusing. If someone wanted to hire you for marketing, the investigations part would make them scratch their heads. And vice versa if they were looking for a private investigator."

"How about Bloom Branding and Bloodhounds?" I said, liking the sound of that.

Brandi scowled. "Do you really want people calling to see if you breed Bloodhounds? Because I don't think they'll know it's another name for a sleuth."

"Ugh." I made a face. "This is hard."

"What about See and Be Seen? Or something catchy like that?" Jonah offered.

Brandi shook her head. "No one will know what you're offering. What about Eye Spy Marketing and Investigation?"

"Too long," Jonah said.

I thought for a moment while Brandi and Jonah read the menu on the wall. The name had to be simple but to the point. An idea popped into my mind. I held up a finger and announced, "I've got it!"

Jonah and Brandi stared at me. So did everyone else in the café.

"How about Bloom Promos & P.I.?" I smiled wide, proud of my revelation. "It pretty much describes both sides of the business."

Brandi laughed. "I like it. It has a nice ring to it."

"I agree." Jonah smiled. "It's perfect."

We moved further up toward the front of the line.

I inhaled the smell of rich coffee and baked goods. "Mmm. I can't believe how lucky we are to work right next to this place."

Brandi frowned. "It's a blessing and a curse. Remember, none of us are making money right now. Coffee is expensive."

"Spoken like a true accountant." Jonah laughed and took out his wallet. "Coffee is on me this morning. I've already landed my first client."

"You have?" I was surprised. How did he have time to work when we were so busy getting our office set up?

"Last week, right after we signed the lease, I ran into the owner of the business next to this coffee shop. You know, the adventure travel agency?"

"Oh, yeah! I saw the display for his river rafting trip in the window," I said.

We reached the front of the line, ordered our drinks, and let Jonah pay.

After we picked up our iced coffees, we re-entered the heat outside.

"Mind if I drop by the travel place to chat with the owner before we head back?" Jonah asked. "I want to see if he had a chance to look at the revisions I sent yesterday."

"No problem," I said. "We should all drop in and introduce ourselves anyway, since we're his new neighbors."

Through the travel shop window, I saw two men in the midst of an argument. The shorter, dark-haired man stormed out the front door. He breezed past us without a word.

We entered before the door could swing shut. The store was cool and inviting. A man climbed up on a chair and tacked a poster to the wall. He glanced at the door as we entered. "Hi Jonah. Sorry about that. That was my cousin. He's a bit ticked off at me today. What brings you in?"

"That's okay." Jonah glanced at Brandi and me. "Ray, I want to introduce you to my friends and colleagues, Brandi Taylor and Clarity Bloom. We're getting our office set up today—just two doors down."

Ray got down from the chair and shook our hands with a firm grip. "Nice to meet you both."

He was sort of handsome, with wiry muscles and skin that had been colored a golden brown by the sun.

Brandi tugged on a curl. I was suddenly aware of her self-consciousness as she adjusted her blouse across her curves. She stood up straighter.

"That's a cool poster," she said brightly.

He gave her a warm smile. "Thank you. It's for my latest river rafting adventure. I can't wait to see how it sells."

"Need some help with marketing?" I asked. "I have a marketing company and would be happy to do an initial social media blast for you—free of charge, of course."

He raised his eyebrows. "Really? Thank you so much. I haven't yet delved into the social media part of marketing. I've been out in the field, testing our high-end adventure packages."

"High-end adventure vacations." Brandi had stars in her eyes. "That sounds amazing."

Ray gave her a crooked smile. "Want to be one of my testers? I'm looking for a few more people to try out my 'Wild River Ride' vacation."

Brandi grinned and looked at Jonah and me. "What do you think, guys? Are you up for an adventure?"

Whatever happened to us being financially responsible? "Can we afford something like that?" I directed my question at her.

Ray put his palm out. "No, no. It's on me. You'll be my guinea pigs. I wouldn't feel right asking you to pay for it. Especially since Clarity is offering to do some social media marketing for me. All I ask is that you post a review on Yelp or Trip Advisor after we return."

Brandi clapped her hands. "Wow! Thank you, Ray. And if you ever need help filing your taxes, I can help with that. I'm a CPA."

"I'll keep that in mind. I've got three slots open for this weekend, if your schedules allow it." He took out a piece of paper. "Read through this and tell me what you think."

Get ready for a thrilling adventure riding the river on a 4-day tour. Participants will depart for the Sauk river Friday morning. We'll spend a night in lavish accommodations at The Black Swan hotel. A 5-course dinner plus drinks and a good night's sleep will prepare you for a wild ride the next morning at dawn. Intermediate rafting skill highly recommended, but not required.

Camping tents and gear are provided. The adventure begins in a challenging river run, followed by two nights of tent camping and hikes. A campfire lunch celebration closes the event on Monday.

After reading through the description, even I was excited, and I wasn't an outdoorsy person.

Jonah's hazel eyes twinkled. "What do you guys think?"

"I'm in." I high-fived him.

"Me too." Brandi flashed a huge smile at Ray.

On our way out the door, Jonah turned. "With all the excitement of the rafting trip, I completely forgot to ask you if you were happy with the revisions I sent yesterday."

Ray nodded. "I reviewed them, and they look great. Can you send it to Astroprints? I use them for all my print materials."

"Done," Jonah said. "I'll send it out later this afternoon after we get our office furniture set up."

"Perfect. Thanks for the quick turnaround." Ray pointed to us. "See you Friday morning. We leave at eight o'clock sharp from the park and ride in Ravenna."

The sudden thought of Pumpkin jarred me. After he'd been kidnapped and almost killed by my serial killer boss, I felt skittish about leaving him all alone. "Wait. I can't leave my cat at home for four days."

Brandi frowned, then pointed her finger at me. "I've got a solution. Why don't you leave Pumpkin with your parents? It's on the way."

I bit my lip. "Maybe. But that means we'll have to meet Ray up in the Skagit Valley instead of going with the rest of the group." I turned to look him. "Is that okay?"

He shrugged. "Sure. Let's meet at the grocery store in Concrete. Is that close enough to your parents' place?"

I nodded. "Just a few miles away, actually. That's perfect."

"It's settled then. Looking forward to Friday." His gaze lingered on Brandi a second longer than necessary.

CHAPTER 2

"Oh, my God." Brandi's expression mirrored the way I felt. "Our office looks amazing."

I was giddy with pride and excitement for our new life. "It does, doesn't it?"

Jonah pointed to his desk. "I love it. Where did you get this furniture? I love how the dark metal legs compliment the rustic barn wood top."

"Thanks. I got it from an estate liquidator. He told me that the furniture was made by a master craftsman who had a furniture design business. When he passed away, he left everything to his new wife—she was about thirty years younger than him. His kids fought tooth and nail to get their share of his estate, but in the end, the lawyers got most of it. They had to sell the business to pay them off." I motioned to the furniture, which included three desks, a coffee table for the seating area, shelving, and a couple of end tables. "It's sad when families fight over money and material things."

Jonah shrugged. "I guess. Families shouldn't fight over trivial things like that. It's not worth it. Though it's their pain, our gain."

All this talk of family reminded me to check in on my parents more often. They drove me a little crazy, but I loved them dearly.

"Did you get the cool rug from the estate liquidator too?" Brandi pointed at the area rug. The bold geometric patterns and colors added to the rustic-urban look of the furniture.

"That came from IKEA." I grinned.

"Trés chic," Jonah said. "I love it. I have some paintings at home that would work well with this look. Want me to bring them in?"

"Absolutely." I glanced at the bare walls. "I didn't have time to look for artwork."

Brandi added, "I don't have any either. When can you bring in the paintings?"

"Tomorrow morning. I'll look through what I have and pick a few that I think will work best."

Brandi clapped her hands. "Awesome. We need to take some pictures then."

"On it," I said. "I'm going to do some social media posts to let people know we're up and running."

Jonah sat down behind his desk and opened his laptop. "I have to send off Ray's designs to the printer. After that, do you want me to work on some logos for you? Accountants usually have boring logos—I can make you something super polished and unique."

"Depends on how much you're charging." Brandi put her hand on her hip.

Jonah laughed. "The first logo is free."

"You're a design pusher, eh? First one is free, then you'll inflate your fees when we're desperate for more." I grinned and sat at my desk as well.

"You've got me all figured out." Jonah smirked.

For the next two hours, we worked in relative silence.

I was deep into researching the steps I had to take to get my private investigator's license when my phone buzzed. It was a text from my brother, Zen.

"Mom and Dad just told me you were getting your P.I. license?" he texted.

I groaned. I shouldn't have said anything to them. "Yes. Since I no longer have a job in corporate America, I have to make a living somehow. I'm doing marketing and private investigations. Just opened an office on 45th in Wallingford." I hit send and waited for his response.

"Clarity. No. I'm calling you," he texted.

Damn.

My phone rang. "Hi, Zen."

"What the hell do you think you're doing?" Zen bellowed.

I winced. "Trying to make a living. How was your day?" I tried to downplay the snark, but it came out snarky nonetheless.

"Clarity," he scolded, "you have no business being a private investigator."

I narrowed my eyes. "And why not? Because I'm a woman?"

Brandi and Jonah shifted uncomfortably in their seats. I turned away from them and faced the wall.

"No. Because the last time you tried to unofficially investigate a crime, you nearly got yourself killed," Zen growled.

"Oh, so it was all my fault that my boss turned out to be a serial killer? And it was my fault he killed my best friend? And kidnapped my cat? And held our parents hostage? You know, Zen, without my help, the police would never have caught Paul. He'd probably still be out killing women." Anger was making my voice pitch higher. I got up and paced behind my desk.

Jonah looked up from his work, his eyes wide.

Brandi raised her eyebrows.

I took a deep breath. "Zen. I'm twenty-seven years old. I'm smart. I'm fairly athletic too. Remember how I stabbed Paul in the side of the neck and then took him down with the self-defense moves Hunter taught me? I can take care of myself."

There was a long silence after my rant.

"I know, I know. I just don't want you to put yourself in danger, that's all. You're my kid sister." His voice was calmer and more measured.

"Your kid sister is strong. I'd like to give this investigations business a try. Will you support me?"

He sighed. "Do I have a choice?"

"Will you teach me how to shoot a gun?"

"No!" His response was immediate. "I don't like that idea at all."

Now it was my turn to sigh. "I understand. I'll take a class or something."

"Clarity." His voice held that warning tone again. "Don't."

This big brother protective stuff was really starting to annoy me. "Was there another reason you called?"

He grunted. "When I talked to Mom and Dad today, they mentioned they needed help harvesting their apples. Can you go up there this weekend and help? I'm booked with a homicide in downtown Seattle."

MARTINA DALTON

"I'm going on a river rafting trip this weekend. I have to stop by Mom and Dad's place to drop off Pumpkin. When I pick him up after the trip, I'll help with the apple picking."

"River rafting, huh? Sounds fun. Wish I could join you. I haven't done that kind of thing since college."

"We're testing out an adventure vacation for a guy who owns a travel agency near our office. If it's fun, maybe we could book another one. You and Hunter could come with us…" I trailed off as I realized he wasn't responding. "Are you there?"

"Yeah. You just want more time with Hunter." Zen's said.

"What?" I tried backpedaling. "No! I just meant that I'd have my friends along, you should feel free to bring yours."

He sighed. "Yeah, right. I know you still have a thing for him, Clarity. But we've already discussed how it is not a good idea for you to get involved with my partner. If you guys broke up, it could affect our working relationship. If he dumped you, it might be difficult for me to have his back one hundred percent, if you know what I mean."

"Do you honestly think you wouldn't protect him if we broke up? You wouldn't do that. You're not that kind of guy."

"Clarity, I know I'm not, but the subconscious is something we can't completely control. Just a hair of hesitation to cover him on my part could cost him his life." Zen's voice was patient, but a hint of irritation crept into his tone as he talked and made me cringe.

"Are you still dating Margaret?" I just had to get that dig in. Zen always played by the rules, but he had broken them when he began dating Margaret. She was Janice's sister—and after Janice had been murdered, Zen had started dating Margaret before the investigation was even over.

He made a huffing sound. "Yes, we are still dating."

I paused long enough for him to jump in.

"But Margaret isn't your partner, and I don't work with her, so it doesn't affect my job," Zen said in triumph.

"I didn't say that," I grumbled. "Since we're on the topic of following your rules about dating, I recall you telling me that you'd never date anyone who was directly involved in an investigation."

"I know, but—" Zen interrupted.

"That's all I wanted to say. Sometimes black and white isn't as clear as you'd like it to be. Real life turns black and white into grays," I said.

He sighed. "I get it. But you promised to stay away from Hunter."

I bit back a bitter response. Clearly, he wasn't willing to be reasonable. "Yes, I realize that. But that doesn't mean I'm happy about it."

"Listen, sis, I don't want to fight. Just promise me that you'll help Mom and Dad this weekend, okay?"

"Okay." I hung up. God, he was so infuriating! We used to have a pretty decent relationship, but it was starting to feel like he was my strict dad and I his naughty teenager.

Brandi and Jonah were watching me silently from their respective desks.

"Sorry, you guys. Brother trouble again." I suddenly realized that having a shared office could diminish our sense of privacy. "We need to think about having a room for phone calls."

Brandi pointed to the back. "We have the conference room. We could use that."

I nodded. "I should've gone in there, but I had no idea Zen was going to bring up the Hunter thing again. He doesn't want me anywhere near him."

Jonah rolled his eyes. "Zen needs to get over himself. Can't he just be happy for you?"

I explained that my brother was worried how my relationship with Hunter would affect their working relationship if anything went wrong between the two of us.

"That still doesn't give him the right to police—no pun intended—your love life." Jonah pushed back from his desk and packed up his laptop. "Sorry about that, girl. I'd offer to take you out for a drink to talk more, but I'm late to a family gathering."

Brandi stood up and began packing up her stuff as well. "Same here. I promised my sister I'd go see a movie with her."

"That's okay. I'll be fine. I have a few more things to do anyway."

Brandi and Jonah left together, letting the door shut softly behind them.

I thought again about Zen's admonishment of me. Not only did he want me to stay away from his partner, he wanted me to drop the whole private investigator thing.

With my jaw clenched tight, I went straight back to the online application to take the private investigators' licensing test. I almost clicked on the option to be armed, but hesitated. The testing was far more extensive for that, and I'd have to learn how to handle a gun. The delay would keep me from getting my license for several more months. Plus, it was more expensive to get an armed PI license. Maybe I wasn't quite ready to own and operate a weapon.

I clicked the option without the firearm and submitted the application.

CHAPTER 3

"Ray asked me out on a date!" Brandi squealed. She was wearing a fitted, floral sundress, and she practically glowed with happiness.

I hugged her. "That's great! He must really like you. He could've waited to take you out after we went on the rafting trip with him."

She blushed. "I ran into him at the coffee shop. We waited in line together, and then he paid for my coffee."

"Is that when he asked you?" I grinned as I slid behind my desk.

"Right before we went back to work. He put his hand on my arm and said, 'You're one of the most beautiful women I've ever met. Would you consider going out to dinner with me tonight?'" Her cheeks flushed again. "He thinks I'm beautiful!"

I smiled. "You are beautiful, Brandi. And that dress is so pretty on you." She did look amazing in it. The cut of the dress highlighted her curves beautifully. "He obviously couldn't resist."

"Aw, thank you, my friend." She sat down at her desk, still grinning.

"Where is he taking you?" I asked.

"To Etta's. I love the seafood there. Turns out, he loves seafood too." She powered up her laptop. "How am I going to concentrate on work when all I can think about is Ray?"

"Hold your horses." I laughed. "You just met him."

"I know it's silly, but this is the first real date I've had in months. I'm just excited."

I stared at my screen. "I know how you feel." Suddenly, I wasn't in the mood to work either. Hunter's face flashed before me—his strong jaw, those dark eyes.

"Clarity?"

"Huh?" I looked up, startled.

"I asked you if you wanted to go for a walk at lunch time. Didn't you hear me?" Brandi gave me a quizzical look.

"Oh, sorry. I was wrapped up in my thoughts. I'd love to go for a walk—but after we eat. I'm already hungry and it isn't even ten o'clock yet."

"Here." She handed me a protein bar. "This should hold you over."

The bell on the door jangled, and Jonah walked in carrying an armload of paintings.

"Let me help you with that." I jumped up and took several of the paintings from his arms. I set them down against the wall. "Wow, Jonah. These are incredible!"

My eyes skipped over the blues, greens, and reds of the abstract patterns. "You should have an art show."

"Thanks, doll." Jonah picked up one of the paintings and held it up to the wall. "What do you think? Should we hang this one here?"

Brandi clapped her hands. "Yes! It's gorgeous. I love how the colors tie in with the rug Clarity bought. Let me get the hammer."

Half an hour later, we stood back to admire his work.

"I'm taking photos now. Let's post pics of our office on our websites and social media." I held my phone up and clicked on the camera app. "People are going to love this."

✷✷✷

The next day, Brandi was floating on air.

"He's such a gentleman!" She fanned herself with a manila folder. "Is it hot in here or is it just me?"

I laughed. "If it wasn't eighty degrees outside, I'd say it was just you. So, Ray's quite the hunk, huh? How was your date?"

"The date was awesome. We have so much in common." Brandi got up and checked the wall thermometer. "Damn. The air conditioning isn't working."

Jonah peeled off his short-sleeved shirt, revealing a tank top with a Bumbershoot logo printed on the front. "We need to get that fixed. I'm melting."

"I got it." I called building maintenance and left a message.

When I hung up, I said, "Back to the date. We want details."

Brandi's grin lit up her face. "He was just the right combination of polite and romantic."

"Where did he take you?" Jonah asked.

"Etta's at Pike Place Market."

Jonah nodded. "One of my faves. I love that restaurant."

"Oh, me too," she said. "We had a lovely dinner, and we talked about everything under the sun. You know, he's obsessed with Baltic music too."

"Really?" I couldn't believe it. Brandi had loved listening to Baltic music since she was a kid, when her parents had taken the family to Estonia on vacation. That was twenty years ago.

She giggled. "I know, right? He even plays the kannel."

"I don't know what that is, but that sounds great."

Brandi's eyes opened wide. "You don't know what a kannel is?"

"Oh, come on." I snorted. "Like the average person knows what that is…"

"Jonah, you know what a kannel is, don't you?" Brandi gave him a hopeful glance.

He shook his head. "I'm sorry to say, no. I don't."

"I can't believe it." She made a tsking sound. "It's an Estonian plucked string instrument. It's making a real resurgence in Baltic music. Here, I'll play you a clip."

"No, no, that's okay," Jonah said a little too quickly. "I'll take you at your word. Besides, I've got work to do." He put in his earbuds and pretended to focus on his screen.

I grinned. "Anyway, it sounds like you two really hit it off."

Brandi sighed. "We did. I can't wait for Friday."

CHAPTER 4

"Come on, Pumpkin, you've got to get in the crate." I avoided getting swiped by my furry angel's paw. Somehow, I managed to push him in and shut the gated door of the cat carrier without losing an eye or a limb.

"Thank God!" I collapsed on the couch in complete exhaustion. "Good grief, kitty. I know you don't like that thing, but do you think I like trying to get you in there?"

My phone buzzed. It was a text from Jonah. "Are you ready to go?"

"Give me a few minutes. I just wrestled my hellcat into his carrier. Can you pick me up in ten minutes?"

"How about Brandi and I come over now so we can help load your stuff outside?" Jonah texted.

"Okay."

Reluctantly, I got off the couch and set the carrier by the door. Next, I grabbed my duffle, sleeping bag, and pillow and set them beside my growling cat.

The doorbell rang.

"Coming!" I ran to fetch the bag filled with treats, kitty litter, and cat food before I answered the door.

Jonah and Brandi stood on the front step, big goofy grins plastered on their faces. They looked like kids heading out to summer camp.

They were both wearing shorts, though Brandi looked a little fancier than Jonah—probably because she had a man to impress.

Jonah, though, was ready for an Indiana Jones adventure. His two-day stubble gave him a rugged appearance. The khaki shirt matched his cargo shorts, and his hat looked like it was straight out of the movie.

"You two look dashing." I smiled and picked up the cat carrier and my duffel bag. "Can you help take this to your car?"

Within minutes, we'd packed up Jonah's small SUV. I sat behind Jonah, with Pumpkin's carrier to my right. He let out a pitiful meow as Jonah started the engine.

"I'm sorry, Pumpkin," I cooed. "You're probably having flashbacks of when Paul kidnapped you."

Brandi turned around in her seat and peered into the carrier. "Poor kitty. You'll have a good time at your grandma and grandpa's psychedelic farm, though."

I rolled my eyes. "I hope Mom and Dad got rid of their weed crop. I don't want Pumpkin to mistake it for catnip."

"Yeah. It would be a shame if he ended up like their first herd of goats." Jonah turned right at the intersection. "Remember? They even invited guests to the critters' funeral."

Brandi snorted.

I shook my head. "Don't remind me."

My mom and dad weren't the typical set of parents. They lived the definition of the hippie lifestyle. It was one of the many reasons my eight siblings and I had tried to distance ourselves from them.

Recently, however, I'd learned that they were real people. People who wanted the same things from life that everyone else wanted—to have enough money to be comfortable, to live true to their own values, and most of all, to be surrounded by people they love. Family.

After Paul had nearly killed them and me, I realized how much family matters. I'd made a vow to myself to give more of an effort to connect with my parents and my siblings. But so far, I'd not done a very good job of it. Zen was the only sibling I had regular contact with, and he was driving me nuts right now.

I stared out the window, lost in thought as I watched the ever-growing traffic roll by at a snail's pace.

Brandi broke the silence. "It's kind of nice that we get to stay in that fancy hotel tonight."

Jonah snorted. "Enjoy it, because on Saturday and Sunday nights, we'll be roughing it."

I groaned. "That's the part I'm not looking forward to. I'm not use to sleeping without a mattress."

"It won't be that bad," Brandi said.

"Says the girl who's floating on air. That love drug is powerful enough to make you forget you'll be sleeping on the hard ground in a tent." I was secretly annoyed that she was free to fall in love with whomever she wished, while I was practically banned from seeing Hunter again.

She glared at me. "Don't be a baby. Sleeping out in nature is a beautiful thing. It's peaceful listening to crickets and the owls in the evening. Don't be such a pessimist."

25

I stewed until we got out of the heavy flow of traffic. Was I being a pessimist? I didn't think so. I was just a little grumpy because I had genuine feelings for a man I would never get to have a relationship with.

By the time we reached the dirt road that led to my parents' house, my grumpiness had dissipated, and the three of us were laughing about the antics of some of our old coworkers.

I got out of the car and stretched my legs.

Mom emerged from the open door of the garden shed, a kid goat trailing her. "Clarity!" She rushed over and gave me a hug. "It's so good to see you, honey."

Mom was still quite the flower child. With her long black hair beginning to gray and her ever-present tie-dye shirt, she was 1969 personified. She even had a daisy tucked behind her ear.

"Good to see you too, Mom."

Pumpkin growled from the back seat.

"What have we here?" Mom rushed forward and brought the cat carrier out of the car. "Well, Pumpkin, how's my little tiger today?"

Pumpkin, who had been surly for the entire car ride, immediately calmed down and was quiet.

"Can I let him out?" Mom fingered the zipper on the mesh door.

"I'm worried he'll have flashbacks of when Paul brought him here," I said.

"Nonsense." Mom set the carrier on the ground and tugged on the zipper. "He loves it here."

I reached out to catch Pumpkin, but he launched himself out of the soft crate with a hiss and landed a few feet from my mom.

Visions of me posting missing cat posters on every telephone pole flashed through my mind.

But instead of running off, Pumpkin stopped to inspect the kid goat that had followed Mom over from the garden.

Pumpkin sniffed the little goat's nose and then began rubbing against its legs, purring.

I raised my eyebrows. Had Pumpkin found his first animal pal?

The goat didn't seem to mind a bit, and happily hopped to the side and waited for Pumpkin to follow. He did.

"Well, would you look at that?" I put my hands on my hips. "He likes goats!"

Mom laughed. "That's Jolie. All the animals around here love her. And I swear, she understands English." She put her hands around her mouth and yelled, "Hey, Jolie! Why don't you take Pumpkin to the barn?" There're a lot of mice in there right now," Mom added out of the side of her mouth.

Jolie made the typical goat maaaa sound and skipped off to the barn. Pumpkin followed closely on her heels.

Jonah got out of the car. "That's amazing! I've never seen a goat follow directions."

Brandi opened the door on her side. "Me neither. You should enter her in one of those TV talent shows."

Mom shook her head. "Nah. She'll get a big head. I want to keep her grounded and down to earth."

I snickered. "Good plan." I opened the back of the SUV and took out a bag of Pumpkin's food, treats, and litter. "Here you go." I handed it to my mom. "Don't overfeed him—he tends to put on weight easily."

"Not here." Mom chuckled. "I'll keep him busy hunting mice."

I looked around the property. "Where's Dad?"

"Oh, he's in the back. He's assembling the greenhouse."

Brandi stared in the direction Mom pointed. "You've got a greenhouse?"

Mom nodded. "Yeah. We finally got the approval to grow medical-grade marijuana. You know, the good stuff."

I closed my eyes and took a deep breath. "Seriously? Didn't you guys learn your lesson with the last crop?" They'd lost an entire herd of goats when the animals got loose and overdosed after eating most of the weed.

Mom glared at me. "You don't need to be so judgmental. That was hard on us too. But, that's why we decided to get a greenhouse. It's goat-proof."

I sighed. "Okay. I sure hope they don't figure out how to break in."

"They won't," Mom said. "I've explained it all to Jolie. She's going to make sure the goats stay away from it."

Jonah covered his mouth to keep from laughing. "This was so worth the stop."

"Would you kids like to come in for some refreshments? I just made some fresh wheatgrass cookies."

My stomach churned. "No, thanks. We better be on our way—don't want to be late to our event."

Brandi and Jonah's shoulders relaxed. I was pretty sure that wheatgrass cookies weren't on their list of favorite foods.

"All right, then. When did you say you'll be back to pick up Pumpkin?" Mom tugged on her long braid.

"On Monday afternoon. I'll call you before we get here."

Just then, Dad appeared from behind the barn carrying a wrench. "Oh, ho, ho! Look who's here! My little girl!" He ran to greet me and picked me up to twirl me around. "You look good, sweetheart. All recovered from the ordeal with the serial killer?"

I wasn't sure how to respond to that. Was I recovered? "Probably," I answered.

"That's good." He greeted Jonah and Brandi and then asked, "Would you kids be willing to help with the apple harvest on your way back?"

Jonah's grin lit up his face. "I would love to."

Brandi and I agreed.

"Awesome," Dad said. "I look forward to seeing you all soon." He headed toward the barn and turned to wave. "Have a safe trip!"

CHAPTER 5

When we got to the Black Swan Hotel, we went to our rooms to change. We were looking forward to the fancy dinner scheduled for early evening. Ray wanted us to get up at first light and had encouraged us to get to bed before nine o'clock.

Jonah's room was right next to the one Brandi and I were sharing, which was good, because we figured we'd be hanging out after dinner.

"Where'd you get the dress?" I said. The dress, basically a red version of the little black dress that every woman had hanging in her closet, fit her perfectly.

Brandi smiled, her dark eyes sparkling. "At Nordstrom. Do you like it?"

"I do. Ray's eyes are going to pop out of his head."

"You look great too, Clarity." She pointed at the burgundy jumpsuit I was wearing. "Is that new?"

I laughed. "No. I've had it for years. When I first got the job at Opulent, I went a little crazy in the wardrobe department. I must have a dozen outfits that I've only worn once or twice."

"Guess those days of wild spending are over for a while, huh? At least until we get a decent number of clients lined up." Brandi applied some red lipstick and blotted it with a tissue. "There! I'm ready. Let's go get Jonah."

***

"Your party is in the Cygnet Room," the host said. "Right this way."

We followed the host through the busy restaurant to a side room where guests were socializing around three large, round tables. The room was beautifully trimmed in dark wood with contrasting white painted walls. Swan emblems were carved into the molding where the trim met the ceiling and each table had a swan-shaped vase bursting with flowers set in the middle.

Brandi caught sight of Ray and immediately went to greet him. I noticed their interaction—she was all smiles and barely contained infatuation. He seemed genuinely happy to see her but was a little reserved—probably because this was a work thing, and he wanted to be professional.

We mingled with our drinks, making small talk as the servers came around with trays of appetizers.

Ray, looking handsome in a dark suit, clinked his glass with a spoon. "May I have everyone's attention, please?"

The chatter died down and we stood to face him.

"First of all, thank you for being guinea pigs in our latest excursion package! It's my pleasure to bring you all together for this inaugural trip. You know, this is our most condensed adventure travel package yet. Up until this point, all our excursions have been a one-week minimum. From photo safaris to Africa to cruises to the Galapagos and Antarctica—our packages are known as the cream of the crop in the adventure travel world."

We clapped along with the other guests.

"In fact," Ray went on, "we've just been voted the number one adventure travel agency in the country by Traveler Magazine!"

"Wow!" Brandi beamed and set down her drink so she could clap with both hands.

"I've looked for ways to expand our customer base and decided that offering a few shorter adventures would be just the thing to open up our services to folks who don't have a lot of time. We're all so busy these days, especially in Seattle, where the high-tech industry rolls along at a breakneck pace. Most people can't afford to take entire weeks, or longer, off work. That's where our shorter travel packages will come in—appealing to upwardly mobile professionals like yourselves who don't have all the time in the world for a fantastic vacation."

We hooted and cheered. He was so right. In the years that I had worked for Opulent, I'd barely taken any time off. And when I did take time off, I was met with double the work when I returned to the office.

Ray pointed to the tables. "We've put your name plates at these three tables. You're seated with your rafting team. Each group has seven vacationers and one rafting guide. This is a chance for you to get to know them before we hit the white water. Enjoy your dinner!"

Once we were seated, the waiters came around with wine, beer, and other drinks.

Brandi was tickled to discover that Ray had assigned himself as a guide for our group, and therefore, was sitting at our table—right next to her.

Jonah was seated next to Brandi. I sat in between Jonah and a guy named Joe, who was a chatty fellow. Throughout the course of the evening, I learned his entire life story.

The food arrived, and I dug in, trying to avoid more conversation with Joe, as he was starting to retell the stories he'd told me earlier.

My eyes were about to roll into the back of my head by the time dessert arrived. Maybe the chocolate mousse would shut him up for a few minutes.

"And my wife, Margie, told me there was no way in H-E-double-hockey-sticks she was going to come on this trip with me," Joe said through a mouthful of chocolate.

He was a tall guy with a bit of a paunch, maybe in his mid-fifties. Though the occasion was semi-formal, he was wearing a pair of rumpled khaki pants and a polo shirt.

"Why won't Margie join you on the trip?" I took a small bite of the mousse, savoring the rich, creamy chocolate.

"She says it's crazy to risk your life for a bit of fun. Her idea of adventure is shopping the anniversary sale at Nordstrom's."

"I see." I took a sip of my wine. "Do you go on lots of trips like this?"

He nodded enthusiastically. "Oh, yeah. I took an early retirement years ago when I sold my construction business. I love doing crazy stuff like this. Last year, I went on the Alaskan survival trip. They flew us in a float plane to a remote location in Alaska, where we had to survive off the land."

"Wow." I set my glass down. "That sounds intense! Weren't you afraid a bear would eat you?"

"Nah. The guides had guns. There were a couple of close calls, but we made it through. Plus, I lost like twenty pounds 'cause all we had to eat we was game and berries."

I snickered. "Well, that's one way to lose weight, I guess. But I'd rather just go to the gym."

He laughed. "We had a great time. Ray's a decent guy. This is my fourth trip with him. There's no other adventure travel business that can even touch his vacation experiences."

"Really? Have you been on any others?"

"Sure. In fact, I went on one that Ray's cousin, Arnold, put together. But it was lame. The guy just doesn't put his heart into it like Ray does. In fact," he said out of the side of his mouth, "Arnold is a guide on this trip. He's the guy with the dark hair and blue shirt over at that table." He waved his hand in the general direction.

My eyes zeroed in on the short, but muscular man. I recognized him as the man Ray had argued with the day we met him at his shop. He didn't look anything like his cousin. Ray was the lean, outdoorsy type. Arnold looked like he spent most of his free time in a gym.

"In fact, I recognize several other folks who are repeat customers," Joe said. "See that tall blonde fetching a glass of wine at the bar?"

The woman was wearing an elegant white dress with a slit up the side, showing off her long, tan legs.

"She looks a little like the supermodel Heidi Klum. Well, if Heidi Klum had the body of an Olympic athlete, that is." I admired her sculpted arms and golden skin.

"Yeah, that's Astrid. And you're right, she is an athlete. She won a bronze medal in the biathlon for Sweden during the last winter Olympics."

"You mean, the sport where they cross-country ski and shoot targets?" My eyes skipped back to her. "That's amazing."

He leaned in closer and whispered, "I think she has a thing for Ray. That's why she keeps signing up for these adventure vacations."

My heart sank. I chanced a look at Brandi, who was gazing at Ray with admiration. What if he preferred the tall Olympic type over the curvy, feminine type?

"Did they ever date?" I whispered back to him.

Joe shook his head. "Not that I know of. Ray likes to keep things professional, so I don't think so."

I wondered if Ray would turn Brandi down because she was a customer. But the look he gave her as she giggled about something he'd just said seemed to indicate otherwise.

"Well, he sure seems to have a great business model put together." I looked at the time on my phone. "Wow. It's nine o'clock already."

Ray looked up from his conversation with Brandi. "Nine? That went fast. We should all get to bed so we can get going in the morning."

"What time are we leaving?" Brandi asked.

I noticed that she'd scooted her chair a little closer to Ray.

"At six o'clock. Breakfast is at five."

Jonah groaned. "Five o'clock? Remind me why I agreed to this again?"

"Oh, you complain, but you looked like a kid in a candy store this morning when we left Seattle," I said.

He laughed. "Okay, okay, you got me. I'm stoked. But five o'clock in the morning is enough to dampen my spirits a little."

"Noted." Ray chuckled and clinked his glass with his spoon. He spoke loud enough for his guests to hear him. "Thank you all for this lovely evening. We should all retire to our rooms for some much-needed rest before our wake-up call. Breakfast is in this room. Meet us, packed and ready to go, in the lobby afterward. We hit the road at six." He raised his glass. "Cheers to new friends and wild adventures!"

"Cheers!" We all raised our glasses.

"I can't wait for tomorrow." Brandi reached over and squeezed Ray's hand.

"Me too," he said.

CHAPTER 6

To voluntarily get out of bed so early seemed like an insane proposition. Brandi and I both had our phone alarms set, and each time we hit snooze, we encouraged the other person to take a shower first.

"You go ahead," I said. "You'll need more time to get pretty for Ray."

She groaned and rolled over. "Dear God. If he saw what I looked like right now, he wouldn't be asking for a second date."

"Go." I pointed toward the bathroom. "Get ready. I'll go after you."

Brandi slithered off her bed and landed on the floor with a thud. "Ow."

I turned onto my side and tried to go back to sleep. But my nerves and excitement for the day of rafting got the better of me.

"Dang it." I sat up in bed and grabbed my phone. It was four-thirty already. "Hurry up in there, Brandi!" I yelled in the direction of the bathroom.

She emerged wearing her cute adventure girl outfit and a towel wrapped around her hair. "Next."

I grabbed my clothes and ran into the bathroom, trying not to stumble into the wall. "I'll be quick. I need coffee."

***

After breakfast, we hurried to pack and meet with the rest of the group. I noticed our group had a mix of people in their mid-twenties to mid-thirties, though there were a few older people too.

Four white vans waited at the entrance of the hotel, the drivers helping people load up. Three vans would be transporting people, the fourth would transport everyone's luggage.

Ray stood on the sidewalk and directed the guests to load quickly.

Jonah, Brandi, and I got into the back of the first van and buckled in.

I was feeling much better after drinking three delicious lattes—the kind where they swirled a leaf pattern in the foam on top. I hoped I wouldn't have to pee anytime soon though.

As we pulled away from the hotel, I put my head on Jonah's shoulder and sighed. "I'm glad we get to do this together, you guys. It's just what we needed after losing our jobs and the stress of setting up our own businesses."

Jonah nodded. "I agree. We deserve a little fun for a change."

Brandi zipped up her North Face jacket and smiled. "This is going to be the perfect day."

***

When we rolled up to the site where the river rafts were waiting for us, I was buzzing with caffeine and excitement.

Growing up, I'd spent a lot of time outdoors. But Mom and Dad never had enough money for us to do adventurous stuff like this. They were too busy starting businesses and then watching them fail. My parents had homeschooled us until we reached high school age, and as a result, we were out of the mainstream of what normal families did for fun.

"Did your families ever go river rafting?" I asked Brandi and Jonah as we climbed out of the van.

"No," Brandi answered promptly. "But we went boating sometimes—even kayaking a couple of times. It was fun."

"We did." Jonah helped a middle-aged woman, who was in our group, out of the vehicle. "But we only did easy runs for beginners. From what Ray said last night, today's run might be a little harder."

"Thanks," the lady said. "I'm Ruth, by the way. This is my first time rafting. In fact, this is my first time doing anything alone." Her face reddened. "I'm newly divorced. Thought I needed something like this to give me confidence."

"Nice to meet you, Ruth." Jonah shook her hand. "I'm sure you'll do great."

We made the rounds of introductions. In our group, there were the three of us, and then Ruth, Joe, Ray, and a young couple on their honeymoon.

"I'm Charles," the wiry young man said. "And this is my wife, Trixie." His goofy grin at using the term "wife" for the first time made me smile.

"Short for Beatrix." The brunette stuck out her hand. "He's the only one who calls me Trixie."

I smiled and shook her hand. "I'm Clarity. Nice to meet you, Beatrix."

Ray took our group to the side, as each guide did with their group. "I'm going to give you an overview of our trip, teach you some techniques, and what to expect on our route today."

He moved us over to a flat area of low brush and forest floor. Small logs had been dragged in to act as practice boats.

Ray pointed to the log we stood next to. "I'd like you all to get into position as if you were on the raft. I'm in the back. I need one person who's done this before and who's good at steering to sit in front."

Charles raised his hand. "I'll do it."

"Great," Ray said. "Let's have three rows of two for the sides."

Once we were settled into kneeling positions, Ray showed us how to paddle to avoid rocks, make it through swirling currents of water, and what to do when there were unexpected obstacles like logs or fallen trees.

The training lasted an hour or so. I was getting anxious to just climb into the raft and give it a try.

"Now, if you fall in," Ray said as everyone scrambled to get into the raft, "we may not be able to haul you back into the boat. But there will be another group behind us, and they can try to pick you up."

"What happens if they can't?" Brandi's brows were furrowed in concern.

I had to admit, I felt the pang of anxiety as well. What if somebody fell out of the raft and no one was able to grab them before they went trundling down the river?

"Don't worry," Ray said. "Our guides are experienced. We know exactly what to do if someone falls in." He chuckled. "We've never lost a customer."

I put my hand to my chest. "Oh, good. That makes me feel a little better."

Ray clapped his hands. "Let's do this!"

The morning's temperature had been cool, but the sun was starting to get warm. I was looking forward to getting on the water, where I was sure the spray would cool us down.

All the rafts were halfway in the water and half on shore. Our group was assigned to the middle raft.

I stepped in awkwardly and tried to keep my balance as I sat in the middle row, on the left side. Wait—was it port side? I knew port was left and starboard was right in boat speak, but did that apply to whitewater rafts? I was too embarrassed to ask, so I just sat down and held on to the side handle while everyone else took their places.

Ray and another staff member pushed us off the sand and into the water. We were on our way.

"Watch out on the left!" Ray shouted from the back. "Use your paddles to keep us away from that rock."

I stuck my paddle out, along with Joe and Beatrix, who were also sitting on the left side, and pushed us away from the large boulder.

"Great job!" Ray called out. "Now, on your right—dig deep to get us out of that dip!"

Jonah and Brandi were on that side and began paddling hard to keep us from plunging into a whirlpool-like eddy.

The boat behind us suddenly came up to our stern and bumped our raft hard. Ray shouted.

I risked a look behind me in time to see a huge rush of water carry the boat behind us right into the back of our raft. Ray toppled off his perch and disappeared into the angry white water.

"Ray!" I leaned over to see if I could spot him.

The guide in the boat behind us yelled, "It's okay! I see him!" He pointed to Ray's red helmet, which had popped up twenty yards upstream. He had his legs out in front of him, just as he'd instructed us to do if we fell in.

Brandi gasped. "Ray!" She tried standing up, but Jonah pulled her back down.

"Sit! He knows what he's doing." Jonah put his hands on her shoulders to prevent her from diving overboard.

Astrid, the Olympic athlete in the boat behind us, had different ideas. She plunged into the water and shot toward Ray. As she attempted to grab his arm, he pushed her away. "I'm fine!" he shouted into the spray.

She was a strong swimmer and once the water flattened out into a calm spot, she swam to shore.

Ray had also reached shore, and was standing at the edge, waiting for our raft to reach the calmer waters. Astrid stood next to him and put her arm around his shoulders.

We paddled to the beachy area and Ray climbed in.

"Are you okay?" Brandi looked stricken. "I thought you were going to drown!"

"I'm fine." He had a sheepish look on his face. "Just goes to show you that even if you have years of experience, Mother Nature calls the shots."

Brandi was visibly relieved. "Thank God you're all right."

"I'm just fine. It takes more than falling out of a raft, or the rapids, to kill me." He chuckled.

The boat that'd been behind us had managed to pull to the bank of the river as well.

"Astrid?" Ray said. "You can rejoin your team. It was reckless of you to jump in after me, but I appreciate your concern. Thanks."

She gave him a coy smile. "You're welcome." Her Swedish accent made her seem exotic and alluring.

Brandi narrowed her eyes. "What was that all about?" she muttered under her breath.

"Looks like the Olympian has a little crush on your man." Jonah waggled his eyebrows.

Brandi whispered, "She better not try to steal him from me. I've been waiting all my life for someone like him."

Ray had been too busy to notice our murmuring. "Charles! Steer us back into the middle, okay? Everyone else, paddle!"

We pulled into the deeper water and soon, we were zigzagging through the turbulent white water once again.

An hour and a half later, we arrived at our destination, thoroughly wet and exhausted, but grinning from ear to ear.

We'd just finished dragging the rafts up the beach, so we could break for lunch. My arms ached and felt like wet noodles. I shook them out to relieve some of the muscle tension.

"That was amazing." Jonah plopped onto the shore.

"Wasn't it?" Brandi glanced over her shoulder and smiled at Ray, who was directing the loading of the rafts.

A dragonfly came flitting by. I watched it hover over the water for a moment before it zipped off into the tall grass at the water's edge.

"This is nice." I sat and pulled my knees up to my chest, hugging my legs. "It's nice to have a break from the city."

Ray came down to sit beside Brandi. "Are you guys ready to eat?"

Jonah grinned. "Of course. Bring it on!"

Ray laughed. "Good. Our lunch is being set up in a meadow, just a short hike from here." He got up and brushed his shorts off. They'd already dried after his spill in the river. "Let's get on the trail."

After bouncing up and down in a raft for the past several hours, my legs felt like Jello on a merry-go-round. The walk felt great after the whole "sea legs" thing wore off. I was starting to feel a little more normal. Except for my grumbling stomach.

"How far is it?" I unbuckled my life jacket and slipped it off my shoulders.

"It's just up there." Ray pointed. "See?"

Ahead, there was a clearing. The trees had given way for a circular meadow populated with wild grasses and low shrubs. As we approached, I noticed a tent had been erected, and there were a few staff members working on what I hoped was lunch.

The scent of sizzling hamburgers and barbecued chicken filled the air.

"Yum!" My stomach let out a loud rumble. "I could eat a horse."

Brandi made a face. "No. You love horses. And you're not French."

Jonah laughed. "Good point."

I frowned. "You know what I mean." And they also knew that I got grumpy without regular feedings. The adrenaline must've kicked my metabolism in gear, because it felt like I hadn't eaten in days.

Brandi grinned. "She's hangry."

I was about to complain when Ray called out to the group. "Food's ready! Come and get it."

"Oh, thank God." I quickened my pace to where the staff was working.

They'd set out folding tables and were beginning to set out trays of hamburgers with all the fixings and grilled chicken.

"If you're vegetarian," Ray said. "We have veggie burgers over on this tray."

"Even if I were vegetarian," I said, "I would probably go for the meat. I think I'm protein-deprived."

I filled my plate with fruit, chips, and a big juicy hamburger. I grabbed a soda and sat down on a stump to inhale my meal. Brandi and Jonah joined me, plopping onto a patch of meadow grass to eat.

For at least five minutes, we were quiet as we gulped down our food.

I finally came up for air and looked down at my plate. It was empty. "Ah." I rested my hand on my stomach. "I feel so much better."

"Me too." Brandi got up and made her way over to Ray.

"Do you see that?" Jonah pointed at her with a carrot stick. "She has totally abandoned us."

I laughed. "Can you blame her? She's got a live one on the line."

Jonah shook his head and grinned. "True. I haven't seen her this happy in a long time. I hope it all works out for her."

The lunch crew began clearing the serving tables. Ray looked up from his conversation with Brandi and shouted, "Head back to the river, everyone! Time to get back in the water."

CHAPTER 7

We'd finished another long run of white water, and Ray's crew had secured the rafts high up on the banks of the river.

Our tents had already been set up a few hundred yards from the water's edge, under the cover of the forest.

As we approached the campsite, I took in the scent of fir and cedar trees. "It smells so nice here."

"It does. Kind of like those evergreen scented candles from the Bath and Body store." Brandi stepped on a twig. The snap echoed off the nearby tree trunks. "There's Ray." She pushed ahead of us and met up with the adventure guide, who was in an intense discussion with his cousin, Arnold. They both stopped in mid-sentence as Brandi sidled up to them.

"I wonder what that's about." I pushed a loose strand of hair out of my eyes. "They seem kind of upset. They must be continuing their argument from a few days ago."

Jonah shrugged. "They're family, so you know how that goes. Sometimes you get pissed off at the ones you love."

"True. I know how that is." With eight siblings, I was well aware of how family dynamics worked. "They're just cousins, but they must be pretty close, considering they're working with each other."

The footsteps crunching on the path behind us made me turn around. "Oh! Hi, Astrid."

"Hello." She gave us hardly any notice as she walked purposefully toward Ray, her blond braid swinging. Once she reached him, she squeezed herself in between him and Brandi.

Brandi's face flushed. She clenched her fists and took a breath through her nose.

Jonah and I scooted in closer so we could hear their conversation. This was getting interesting.

"Hi, Ray. That was a great run." Astrid touched his arm.

"Yeah." Ray subtly took a step back. "It was pretty great." His eyes flicked to Brandi as he gave her a reassuring smile. "Tomorrow's run will be even better."

Astrid's friendly expression hardened as she followed Ray's gaze. Her blue eyes seemed to frost over for just a moment before she regained her composure. "I'm looking forward to it." She tugged on Ray's arm. "Can you show me which tent I'll be in?"

He nodded. "I might as well let everyone know all together so I don't have to repeat myself." He clapped his hands. "Attention, everyone! We've got six tents set up—three green ones for the women, and three blue ones for the men. Feel free to choose a tent. Your bags and sleeping bags have been placed by that large boulder next to the alder tree." He pointed at a spot off to the side. "Let me know if you have any questions or concerns."

Jonah spotted his stuff right away and dashed off to a tent where some of the guys were heading.

Brandi and I found our stuff and turned to assess our options.

The green tents were situated further into the trees on the left. The men's tents were to the right.

I shivered in my wet clothes and was relieved to see a large campfire circle was set up in the center, outlined with big river rocks. Logs were set up around the outskirts of the circle for seating.

We watched Astrid go into the first tent.

"Let's take the second one." Brandi marched past me and disappeared into the opening of the tent.

I followed on her heels and ducked under the flap.

The tent was spacious, and if my calculations were correct, there'd be four women per tent. Brandi was unrolling her backpack to one side, and I set my stuff down next to her.

"Smart move picking a different tent than Astrid's," I whispered.

"I can't stand that Amazonian woman. She's trying to get her hooks into Ray."

Unrolling my sleeping bag and flopping down on it, I said, "She's pretty obvious about it. I wonder what he thinks of that."

She gritted her teeth. "I don't know. But how can I compete with her? She's like if America's Top Model and American Ninja Warrior had a baby."

"More like Swedish Ninja Warrior," I said.

Sighing, she leaned back on her heels. "She's everything I'm not."

"Brandi, he clearly is interested in you. You're gorgeous, smart, and fun. How could he not like you?"

Ruth and Beatrix entered the tent put their stuff down and started to get unpacked.

I turned to them and grinned. "I'm glad we're bunking with you guys."

They returned my smile.

"Same," Beatrix said. "This will be like a sleepover!"

Ruth laughed. "I haven't been on a sleepover since I was sixteen. And let me tell you, that was in the Jurassic period."

Brandi giggled. "Oh, stop it. You're not that old."

Ruth snorted. "Whatever you say."

Beatrix stopped what she was doing and sniffed the air. "Did they start cooking already? That smells amazing."

"Let's go see if they need help." I ducked under the flap and emerged outside, taking in the scent of heavenly food.

Joe, my friend from our table at the Black Swan Inn, was hovering near the fire pit, watching the chicken sizzle on the metal grill. He rubbed his hands together. "I can't wait to eat."

More heads peeked out of the surrounding tents as the smell of food filled the forest air.

People began inching closer to the where the cooking was happening, as Ray's crew tended to the Dutch ovens filled with roasting potatoes. Some of the big cast iron pots contained desserts, which I guessed from the aroma of bubbling berries.

"Is that blackberry cobbler?" Brandi sniffed the air. "God, that smells amazing."

My stomach rumbled in agreement. I scurried over to one of the chefs. "Is there anything we can help with?"

The tall man smiled and said, "No, we've got everything under control. Though, if you'd like to direct people toward the drinks, that would be great." He pointed to two large coolers.

"Got it." I began herding folks toward the cold drinks and grabbed a beer for myself.

Once I'd settled on the logs surrounding the firepit, I let the heat of it warm my body. I sighed with pleasure as the chill of the river dissipated. I hadn't even realized how cold and wet I'd been until now.

Brandi and Jonah joined me, and we stared into the flames as we sipped our drinks.

"This is the best." Jonah's serene smile made him look so young. Like all the stress we'd been through in the last couple of months had been erased.

I nudged him with my elbow. "It is. We're lucky to be here together."

Brandi had scanned the area and had locked eyes onto Ray, who was talking to Joe, Astrid, and a few other people from the other rafts. "Excuse me a moment." She got up and made her way to the group.

"She's got it bad for him." Jonah grinned and ran his hand over his stubble.

I laughed. "She does. I hope it all works out for her."

The minute Brandi joined the small group, Astrid stepped closer to Ray and giggled at everything he said.

"Gross." I narrowed my eyes. "She is really horning in on Ray. I hope Brandi doesn't punch her. Or maybe I should…"

Jonah snorted. "Yeah, Astrid is trying way too hard. It's kind of pathetic, if you ask me."

"Ray doesn't seem to be taking the bait. Why do you think that is? She's certainly beautiful and strong. And she's super into him." I put my empty bottle down next to me.

"I don't know. She's probably not his type." He watched Ray smiling down at Brandi. "But Brandi is. Obviously, he has excellent taste."

I smiled. "It makes me like him even more. He's a nice guy. Want another beer?" I stood up.

"Yeah, I'd love one."

I took our empties to the recycle bin next to the coolers and grabbed two cold brews.

"Thanks." Jonah took the beer from me and twisted off the cap.

A big guy from the first raft joined the group talking with Ray.

"Who's that guy?" I studied the man's broad shoulders. "He looks like he spends hours in the gym."

"I talked to him for a few minutes last night. His name is Carlson. He's actually a venture capitalist. He said he's thinking of buying into Ray's company to make it a nationwide chain."

"Interesting." I wrinkled my nose. "I wouldn't have pegged him for a financial dude."

Jonah nodded. "Me neither. He seems kind of aloof, though. And if he was wearing a suit, I think it would change our perspective."

"True. What about the woman standing behind him? What's her deal?" A lanky woman with dark hair stood behind Carlson.

"That's his wife, Marlena. She doesn't say much." Jonah took a bite of his grilled chicken.

I watched as she seemed to shrink behind her husband. When he turned to ask her a question, she answered him in a one-word response, barely making eye contact. She looked like a beaten dog who was careful not to anger her master.

"I don't think I like him," I said.

Jonah nodded. "I'm with you. He seems like an ass."

Ray's cousin, Arnold, joined the group, squeezing himself in between Ray and Astrid. She scowled at him but moved over to make room.

"What is up with Arnold?" I unzipped my fleece jacket a bit to let the fire warm my skin. "He and Ray don't seem to get along very well."

Jonah shrugged. "I overheard a conversation between Arnold and Joe this morning while we were shuffling our gear. Arnold has been trying to convince Ray to make him a partner in Ray's business. He feels Ray owes it to him."

"Interesting. Why?"

"I don't know," Jonah said. "Something about Ray inheriting some money from their grandfather which he used to start up the business."

"Didn't Arnold inherit some too?"

"Apparently, Ray is a favorite and got more money than Arnold. But that's all I heard. I don't know any of the other circumstances."

Ray whistled loudly. "Food's done! Come and get it!"

CHAPTER 8

I was so full I could hardly climb into the tent. Once I got inside, I lay flat on my outstretched sleeping bag and groaned. "Oh, God. I don't think I'll need to eat again for at least a couple of days."

Brandi giggled. "Me too. But I bet we'll be hungry again after tomorrow's whitewater run."

"Doubtful. Just the thought of food makes me want to hurl."

Ruth and Beatrix entered the tent, each holding their stomachs.

I laughed as they repeated what I'd just said about food, almost word for word.

"Beatrix, you and Charles just got married, right?" I rolled over on to my side.

The pretty, young woman gave me a wistful smile. "Yep. He's wonderful, isn't he?"

"I'm sure he is. But why on earth did you choose a whitewater rafting trip for your honeymoon? You can't even sleep in the same tent."

Brandi sat up and propped her backpack behind her back. "When I get married someday, I'm never going to leave the honeymoon suite. Champagne and lots of…" Her words trailed off and her eyes twinkled.

Beatrix laughed. "Oh, don't worry. We plan to do plenty of that later. After this trip is over, we're heading off on a romantic vacation to Hawaii."

"Well, that's a relief," Ruth said. "I was starting to worry about you and Charles. When my ex and I got married, we humped like rabbits."

"Ruth!" Beatrix covered her mouth but couldn't suppress her laughter. "I can't believe you just said that."

Ruth shrugged. "The older I get, the less of a filter I have on my mouth. With age comes the inability to keep one's mouth shut."

I clapped my hands. "I love that. Can't wait to get older."

Brandi yawned. "Well, you're only twenty-seven. You've got plenty of years left to keep your mouth shut."

"Maybe now that I've shared that nugget of wisdom," Ruth said, "you can all start speaking your mind earlier. Now that I'm divorced, I'm finding that I'm speaking my mind more and more. It feels good."

I reached across Brandi to pat Ruth on the shoulder. "You're my new hero. Thanks for sharing that."

Ruth blushed. "You're welcome. Now, let's get some sleep. Tomorrow is going to be a doozy of a day."

✳✳✳

"I have to pee." Brandi sat up and rubbed her eyes. "I don't want to go alone. I might get lost. Will you come with me?"

55

My eyelids were glued together and it took effort to pry them open. "Ugh. What time is it?"

Brandi checked her waterproof wristwatch. "Six o'clock."

"I hate six o'clock." I rolled over to my other side. "You won't get lost. Remember it's that wooded area near the river where our rafts are? We went there last night. Go back down the trail and look to the left side. That's where the women go and to the right is where the guys go."

"Wandering in the woods alone to pee is scary—even in the daylight," Brandi whined. "This is the part about camping that I don't like."

I groaned. "You'll be fine. There's toilet paper in a box near the coolers."

"Oh, God." Brandi extricated herself from her sleeping bag.

I could feel her eyes on me, so I rolled over. "What?"

"Will you go with me?" After a long pause, she offered, "Please?"

I let out a dramatic sigh. "Oh, all right. But you owe me."

She grinned. "I'll buy you a drink when we get back home."

"Deal." I wiggled out of my warm sleeping bag and winced at the cold air hitting my exposed skin.

"Make that two drinks." I grabbed my fleece jacket and climbed out of the tent after Brandi.

The morning light played on the various trees and bushes where the sun had penetrated the forest canopy. The crisp air felt clean and fresh as I inhaled deeply through my nose.

Brandi rubbed her hands together. "Brrr. Let's hurry so we can get back into our warm sleeping bags."

I walked quietly to the box near the coolers and opened it. "Yuck." I brushed an earwig off a roll of toilet paper and tucked the roll under my arm. "I hate bugs."

The instructions taped to the lid in the box said to put the used toilet paper in a Ziplock bag. We had to put the bag in the garbage receptacle back at camp when we were done. Gross. But I figured all us river rafters would leave quite a mess if we didn't clean up after ourselves. I grabbed two Ziplock bags, handed one to Brandi, and shut the lid, careful not to make a loud noise.

The sounds of the forest were comforting. Twittering birds serenaded us from every branch, like a surround-sound Discovery Channel show.

We tiptoed out of the campsite, careful not to make any rustling noises. The other campers deserved to get as much sleep as possible before the challenge of the whitewater course began. Heading down the path that led to the "bathroom" area, we walked in comfortable silence.

Once we got there, Brandi spotted a tall shrub closer to the riverbank. "That's my stall over there." She handed me a strip of toilet paper. "Meet you back here when you're done."

"Thanks." Since I was already out in the cold, I thought I might as well go too. I hunted around for a good spot and finally found one near a large tree surrounded by a clump of bushes. I turned around in a circle, making sure there was no one else around.

A squirrel skittered up a tree and scolded me for invading his territory. "Sorry, but you'll have to avert your eyes, furry friend."

He peeked around a branch and glared at me.

"Shoo!" I waved him away and watched as he ran off.

With my pants scooched down around my ankles, I carefully thought through the laws of physics to avoid peeing on myself.

Finally, I had it figured out. I wriggled my yoga pants down and was in mid-stream when an ear-piercing shriek broke the stillness of the morning. My heart stopped beating momentarily, and I floundered to maintain my balance.

Was that Brandi screaming? Had she stepped on a snake or run into a spider web?

"Brandi!" I yelled. "Are you okay?" I regained my balance, finished my business, and hurriedly pulled up my pants.

"Help! Someone, help!" Brandi screeched.

I ran toward her voice, nearly falling over a tree root on the way. "I'm coming!"

A branch slapped me in the face, and I pushed it out of the way, only to have it slap the back of my neck as it snapped back into place.

I ran toward my screeching friend. She was bent over near the tall bush she'd pointed at earlier. Her hands covered her mouth and her eyes were wide open in shock.

"Brandi? What is it?" I approached her cautiously. My eyes scanned the ground looking for a snake or some other kind of forest vermin.

She pointed a shaking finger at a crumpled form on the other side of a fallen log. "Over there."

What was that? A pile of clothes?

I approached the bundle cautiously.

From the direction of the campground, voices were raised and suddenly, people from our rafting party emerged through the thicket.

The dark figure on the other side of the log lay face-down and motionless. To the right of his body, lay a wooden oar. Congealed blood coated the blade.

A crimson puddle stained the leaves and dirt around the man's head.

Though I couldn't see his face, I knew he was dead.

CHAPTER 9

The pounding of feet on the forest path grew louder. A herd of adventurers burst through the brush.

"What happened?" Joe pushed his way to the front of the pack. "We heard screaming."

Brandi turned to him, her face streaked with tears. "There's a—a body."

The campers murmured among themselves and craned their necks, trying to catch a glimpse of the body.

Joe rushed forward. "What? Where?"

I flung my arm out. "Stop. We don't want to disturb the crime scene."

"What are you, some kind of cop?" Carlson, the big venture capitalist guy asked.

My face flushed. "No, but I'll be getting my P.I. license soon. And I recently helped the police with an investigation."

"Well, good for you. I feel so much safer now." He smirked. "Who's the dead guy?"

"I don't know. He's face down."

Ray wriggled his way from the back of the crowd. "Let me see." He approached Brandi and me and peered over the log. His face drained of color. "Oh, my God," he whispered. "It's Arnold, my cousin."

I gave him a sharp look. "How do you know?"

He covered his face with his hands. "Oh, God. No."

Brandi touched his arm. "How do you know it's Arnold?"

"His jacket. I gave it to him last week." He kneeled down next to his cousin and carefully checked his neck for a pulse. Not finding one, he leaned back on his heels and shook his head. "He's gone."

"I'm calling the police." I dug my phone out of my pocket and checked for a signal. I barely had one bar. I dialed 911 and hoped it would go through.

When the call finally got picked up the dispatcher, I panicked when I couldn't give the emergency operator an address. "I don't know where we are—we're on a rafting trip! But someone has been murdered. Help us!"

Ray motioned for me to give him the phone. "Let me talk to them."

While he was describing the area to the operator, Brandi clutched my arm. She was shaking so badly, I could feel the vibrations all the way down my torso to my legs.

"Brandi, I think you're going into shock. Let's sit down over there." I looked at the sea of concerned faces. "Does someone have a bottle of water they can spare?"

Jonah, still in his long johns, yelled. "I'll get mine!" He jogged back toward the campsite.

Turning my attention back to Brandi, I helped her sit with her back against a Douglas fir tree. "Take deep breaths. Help will be here soon."

I put my hand on her shoulder. "Breathe."

She took some deep breaths, until finally, her trembling subsided somewhat.

"That's it." I patted her shoulder. Once I knew she was improving, I glanced around at the crowd of campers.

Astrid sat on the forest floor, visibly shaken. She put her hand to her neck, feeling for something at her collar bone. "I think I lost my necklace," she muttered.

Carlson stood behind her and stroked the top of her head. "Don't worry about it."

Ray was keeping everyone away from the body while he talked to the 911 operator.

Why was Carlson so touchy-feely with Astrid? Where was his wife? I searched the crowd and found his significant other, Marlena, standing off to the side, her eyes narrowed as she watched her husband with Astrid.

Jonah appeared, huffing from his run back from the campground. "Here." He knelt next to Brandi and handed her the water bottle. "Drink."

"How is she?" he whispered.

Brandi took a small sip and hiccupped back a sob.

"Better, I think." I rubbed her back.

"You know I can hear you, right?" Brandi said.

I smiled. "You are feeling better. I'm so glad. We were worried."

After what seemed like forever, sirens wailed faintly in the distance. A bird rustled a bush nearby and fluttered off to the branches above.

"The police will be here any minute. How far are we from the road?" I looked at Jonah, as if he would have the answer.

He shrugged. "Why are you asking me? My sense of direction is almost as bad as yours."

"Well, I hope they aren't too far. Or it might take a lot longer for them to reach us." I sunk down into the roots of the tree and hugged my knees.

The sirens grew closer. In the distance, voices of men and a few women echoed through the forest.

"Over here!" one of the campers yelled.

Radios crackled. The voices burst through the brush. Six police officers and several EMTs approached us.

"Over here, officers." Ray waved his arm in the air. He spoke to the 911 operator. "They're here. Thank you." After he'd ended the call, he motioned for me to retrieve my phone. When his gaze landed on Brandi, his eyebrows furrowed with concern. "Is she okay?"

I took the phone from him. "I think she'll be fine. But she's pretty shaken up. We should have one of the EMTs look at her."

Ray talked to a man wearing a dark blue uniform with a medical insignia printed on the pocket and pointed to Brandi.

Jonah stayed with her while the EMT took her blood pressure and asked her questions. I wandered over to where Ray was standing with the police.

"Who found the body?" A plain-clothes cop peered over the log.

"Brandi did," I pointed to my friend. "She screamed, and I came running."

The tall but sturdy man studied me. "Was there anyone else around when you two discovered it?"

I shook my head. "No. Just us, as far as I know." But that made me wonder. Was the killer hiding behind a bush when we came upon Arnold? I shuddered to think that we might've happened if he'd been hiding behind a bush when Brandi discovered the victim. I replayed the scene in my head. I didn't remember hearing any footsteps running away. Maybe Arnold had been killed hours ago, but no one realized he was missing.

"All right," the man in charge said. "I'll need to talk with all of you while we wait for the medical examiner to get here. Let's start with the woman who first discovered the body."

While the detective in charge talked to Brandi, Jonah joined me and Ray.

"I need to call our drivers and ask them to pick up our equipment here." Ray raked his fingers through his hair. "I'm cancelling the rest of the trip."

"Of course." I nodded.

"I need to go back to the campsite to get my phone." Ray turned toward the path and was only a few feet along when the detective shouted at him.

"Sir, you can't leave yet! In fact, no one leaves here until you've been interviewed."

"Crap." Ray turned around. "Clarity, can I borrow your cell again?"

"Sure." I handed it to him.

Once Ray was out of earshot, Jonah said, "Who do you think would want Arnold dead?"

"I don't know. But I did see Ray arguing with him last night."

"Me too," Jonah said. "I hope that doesn't make him a suspect."

"Everyone is pretty much a suspect right now." But I did worry about Ray. Had he been angry enough with his cousin to kill him? And what were they arguing about?

Brandi stood up and took a sip of water. The detective had finished interviewing her.

"Ma'am," he said as he walked toward me. "You were the second person on the scene. I'd like to talk to you next."

"That's fine with me. Excuse me a minute, Jonah."

The man stuck out his hand. "I'm Detective Reilly."

"Nice to meet you, Detective. I'm Clarity Bloom. My brother, Zen Bloom, is a homicide detective with the Seattle PD."

He raised his eyebrows. "I know Zen! Good guy. I worked with the Seattle PD up until last year when I decided the big city was too chaotic for me. I'm glad you know a little about how this process works."

I nodded. "I'm somewhat familiar. I helped my brother with a case just a few weeks ago."

"Helped? How exactly did you do that?" He seemed amused.

I resisted the urge to punch him. Did he think I was making stuff up in order to make myself look important?

"Actually, my best friend was murdered. I helped find the killer after he kidnapped my parents and took my cat hostage. He's awaiting trial now."

Detective Reilly's mouth dropped open. "Are you talking about the Paul Walker case?"

"Yep. Paul was my boss."

"Our department helped with the takedown of that SOB."

I studied his face. He was in his forties—handsome, but in a rugged way. Square jaw, a tinge of red to his light brown hair, and piercing blue eyes. "Then, you may have seen me. I was the woman Paul was dragging off to the forest."

His eyes widened. "Yeah, I do remember you now." His eyes flicked to the area where the body lay. "Curious that you're involved in another murder case, just weeks after the one you just described."

I shifted my weight from one foot to the other. "I guess that is a little weird."

He grunted and jotted something down in his notebook. "What can you tell me about finding the body?"

"Brandi asked me to come with her to find the, uh, bathroom area. I didn't want to go, but she guilted me into it."

He chuckled. "Go on."

I explained how she'd screamed, and I'd come running, only to discover the lifeless form on the other side of the log.

"Was Brandi anywhere near the victim? Did she touch him?" he asked.

"No, she was standing a few feet away. She was too stunned to go near him."

"And do you know who the victim is?" he asked.

"Ray identified him as his cousin, Arnold."

"Last name?"

I shrugged. "I don't know Arnold's last name. I barely talked to him."

"Do you know if anyone seemed unfriendly toward Arnold? Any strange behavior with Arnold and others on the trip?"

I swallowed hard. This was the part I was worried about. I didn't want to get Ray in trouble, but…

"Clarity?" The detective urged me on.

I sighed. "I did see him arguing with Ray last night. But I don't think Ray would hurt anyone, let alone his own family."

"Have you known Ray long?"

"No. We just met him earlier this week."

"Who's we?"

"Brandi, Jonah, and myself. We have a business next to Ray's in Seattle."

He jotted more notes down. "Do you know what Ray and Arnold were arguing about?"

"I have no idea. Maybe Brandi knows more."

"Why would your friend know more?" He looked up from his notes.

"Because she and Ray kind of like each other." God, why was I telling him all this? I might as well just throw my friends under a bus. Maybe the detective had the same effect on me as truth serum.

"How long have they been dating?" Detective Reilly asked.

"They've only been on one date."

"Was there anyone else who didn't like Arnold?"

I surveyed my rafting friends. My eyes lingered on the place where Arnold's body lay silent and still. "I don't know. He didn't seem like the warmest person, you know? The only one I talked to who knows him is Joe. And I think Astrid knows him too. Both Joe and Astrid have been on previous trips with Ray's company. Joe mentioned that Arnold had tried starting a company like Ray's, but he wasn't successful."

Detective Reilly nodded as he took more notes. "Can you think of anything else? Any other details or information about Arnold and his relationship with the other people on the trip?"

"No."

"Thank you, Clarity. You've been very helpful. Here's my card in case you think of anything else."

I took it from him and put it in my pocket. "Thank you. I hope you find out who did this."

He met my eyes. "Me too."

CHAPTER 10

Everyone had been interviewed, and we'd all been sent to pack up our stuff. Ray's employees took down the tents and loaded the food into wheeled carts. My stomach rumbled thinking about our missed breakfast, but it wasn't appropriate to mention food at this time.

The victim had been collected by the medical examiner, but the police were still examining the crime scene.

"The vans are here, waiting on the road. Please follow me. My crew will take care of the tents, rafts, and equipment." Ray pointed us to a path that led away from the river.

"Come on." I took Brandi's hand in mine and tagged along after Ray. Jonah followed at our heels.

The trip was supposed to have momentarily taken us away from the stress of the city. Instead, it had turned into something far more stressful than starting a new business.

Jonah, noticing that Brandi and I had gone quiet, tried to distract us with funny stories from his childhood.

"And then my dad made us clean the entire garage. That was the last time we ever whined that we were bored." Jonah chuckled. "Except my youngest sister, Ellie. She didn't learn as fast as the rest of us did and ended up having to wash the boat a couple of times. She's not the brightest bulb in the chandelier, if you know what I mean."

I smiled. Brandi's face remained blank.

Jonah frowned.

"Thanks for trying," I mouthed to him. I hoped he didn't take it personally. She was still suffering the after-effects of discovering Arnold's body.

Once we got into the back seat of one of the vans, I felt a weight lift off my shoulders. Soon, all of this would be behind us and we could move on with our lives.

The driver let the engine idle while we waited for everyone to finish talking to the police and then load into the other vehicles. Ray was sitting in the front passenger seat talking in low tones to the driver. Beatrix, Charles, and Ruth sat quietly in the row in front of us.

"Maybe our next trip should be somewhere warm and exotic. A place where we can lay out on the beach and drink tropical drinks with the little umbrellas in them." I buckled my seatbelt and hoped Brandi would say something cute and funny, like she always did.

Jonah hesitated a moment, probably waiting for a response from Brandi too. "Yeah, that sounds like a much better option than this." Then he whispered so only I could hear, "And I don't think there are any dead bodies sunbathing on white-sand beaches."

"So true," I whispered back.

I rubbed Brandi's arm, hoping to get a response. "Are you okay?"

She shrugged. "I guess."

"That must've been so scary to come upon Arnold like that. I'm sorry it was you and not me."

She shot me a glance. "What? What do you mean?"

"When Hunter and Zen took me along to a crime scene in Ballard—before we knew that Paul was a killer, I saw something gruesome." I flashed back to the severed leg laying in an alley next to a dumpster. "And I was surprised that I was more curious than grossed out. It was almost like I was watching a movie instead of experiencing it in real life."

Brandi blinked. "What did you see?"

I shook my head. "I don't think you want to know. Let me just say that it was awful."

"But you didn't panic? Or throw up?"

"Nope. I almost feel bad about that. I mean, the normal thing would be to have the reaction you're having, right? Maybe that makes me some kind of outlier. I should be sick to my stomach and traumatized. But I'm not."

Brandi laid a hand on mine. "No. It just means you have the ability to analyze a horrible event. I think it means that you're suited to this type of work."

"PI work?

She nodded. "Exactly. You're meant to do it."

"Well, maybe not in this instance. No one has hired me to find out who killed Arnold. The police are handling that just fine."

"True." Brandi studied the back of Ray's head. "I feel bad for Ray. Arnold was his cousin. What should I say to him?"

"Tell him you're sorry for his loss. Hug him and tell him you're there for him."

She squeezed my hand. "Yeah. This whole traumatic thing is not about me. It's about someone losing his life. For Ray, it's about the loss of a family member." She was quiet for a moment. "It actually makes it easier to put the focus on Ray and his experience rather than focusing on my own reaction to finding Arnold's body."

The van's engine was loud enough that it covered our quiet conversation. But Ray must've felt our eyes on him.

He turned around in his seat to look at us. His face was pale and drawn, and the smile he normally wore was nowhere in sight. "You okay back there?"

Brandi leaned forward. "We're all right. The better question is, how are you? I'm so, so sorry about Arnold."

"Thank you, Brandi. I don't know what to think. What happened today was quite a shock. I don't know what I'll tell the family."

"Was Arnold on your mother's side or your father's side?" I wasn't sure why I was asking. But I was starting to feel a tickle of curiosity deep down in my gut.

"On my mother's side. Arnold is the son of my mom's sister, Peggy."

"Are your families close?"

"Yeah." His face grew even paler. "Growing up, we lived right next door to Aunt Peggy and her kids. Arnold had two older sisters. They were always over at our place. Arnold was like a brother to me when we were little. Well, except he was like that annoying little brother who was always tagging along with you and your friends." He chuckled, and then shook his head. "I can't believe he's gone."

"So, did you two get along as adults?"

Brandi shot me a warning look. "Clarity," she hissed. "What are you doing?"

My cheeks flushed. "Sorry, Brandi. I can't help it."

"We got along," Ray said. "For the most part. Every now and then, he gets... got... on my nerves." He turned his body back around and stared out the window while the others climbed into the van.

I played back the scene in my head during last night's dinner. The two men arguing by the campfire. What were they angry about? I wanted to ask more questions, but the daggers Brandi was shooting at me made me swallow my words.

Jonah, in the seat next to me, looked nervously from me to Brandi. "We're returning two days early. Do you guys want to go straight home once we pick up the car at the hotel?"

Wistfully, I thought there would be nothing better than to go home and forget all this happened. But I'd made a promise. "Would you guys be okay with helping my parents harvest apples? We can help them make cider too, if you're up for it. Hopefully, we can stay overnight in their bed and breakfast."

Brandi perked up a bit. "Yes! Doing something chill sounds great right now."

"I'd love to help." Jonah shifted in his seat and let his head rest against the headrest.

Once we got back to the hotel. We piled out of the van. The other passengers, Beatrix, Charles, and Ruth had slept during the trip back. Their faces bore the seatbelt imprints to prove it.

We hugged them goodbye and joined Ray and the driver.

"Thank you for the, uh, rafting trip," Jonah said awkwardly as he shook Ray's hand.

Ray looked down at his feet. "Sorry it turned out like this. I don't know what to say, except that I'm devastated."

"We're the ones who are sorry." Brandi hugged Ray. "Please let us know if you need anything."

He nodded, not meeting Brandi's eyes. "Will do."

Brandi seemed crushed. I could tell she desperately wanted to do something, but there wasn't a thing she could do to make it better.

Not knowing the right thing to say, I gave Ray a simple thank you, and we gathered our packs and found Jonah's car.

The silence enveloped us on the drive to my parents' house.

I struggled to gather my thoughts. Unless a random stranger had killed Arnold, someone in our rafting party was a murderer.

CHAPTER 11

The sun was shining brightly by the time we reached Mom and Dad's house.

Jonah pulled into the graveled parking space next to the bed and breakfast and turned off the engine.

The front door of the main house opened, and Mom stuck her head out. "Well, my goodness! What are you doing back so early?" She stepped outside and greeted us as we tumbled out of the car.

"Our trip was cut short," I said. "One of the rafting guides was killed."

Mom grabbed my arm. "Oh my God! What happened? Did he fall overboard?"

"No." I paused. "He was murdered." My stomach dropped as I thought about the gruesome discovery Brandi and I had made in the early hours of the morning.

"I can't believe it." Mom dropped my arm. "That's terrible. Did they get the killer?"

"Not yet," Jonah said. "We were all interviewed by the police, but so far, no arrests have been made."

"None that we know of, anyway," I added.

"You should call your brother." Mom picked up my backpack and set it on the porch. "Maybe he can come out here and help with the investigation."

"It's not his jurisdiction, Mom."

"I know. But maybe there's something he can do? I don't know. But, in any case, you're all welcome to stay here. We just had a cancellation for a party of four, and the inn is empty. Come on. Let's get your stuff inside."

We followed her through the door.

"Girls, you can take the two ground-floor rooms. Jonah can take one of the rooms upstairs. First door to the left, Jonah," Mom called to him as he made his way upstairs.

"Thanks." I opened the door to my room. Inside, the walls were painted a calming blue. I was pleasantly surprised at the elegance of the décor, considering I'd expected to see something a little more 60s or 70s tie-dye-themed.

The queen-size bed's plush white comforter looked soft and inviting after a night of tent-camping. I sat down and scooted my back against the oversized blue and white pillows. "Nice," I said out loud.

"You like it?" Mom stood in the doorway. "Your sister, Henna, did all the interior decorating."

That made a lot more sense. Henna was an artist. "Well, she did a wonderful job."

"I think so too." Mom sat on the end of the bed. "Are you kids going to stay to help with the apple harvest?"

"Of course!" I got up and put my shoes back on. "We'll help with the cider production too. But first, I'm going to take your advice and text Zen about this murder. I just want to get his take on the situation."

"Excellent idea. I'll just head to the barn to get out the garden gloves and ladders."

"Okay, meet you there."

I texted Zen and explained about the murder.

His response came back almost immediately. "Figures that you'd get involved in another murder investigation."

"Hey!" I texted back. "That's not fair. I didn't choose to get involved." As usual, Zen was laying blame on me when I deserved absolutely none.

"Yeah, yeah, I know. I'll call the police department up there. A guy I know there used to work with the Seattle PD."

"That's right. One of the detectives I talked to said he knew you." I put the phone in my pocket and went outside to meet my mom.

Brandi and Jonah were already standing on ladders, picking apples.

"Hi honey," Dad said. He ran to hug me. "I heard the news. I'm so sorry someone in your rafting party was killed. Are you all right?"

"Thanks, Dad. I'm fine." I glanced at my friends, absorbed in the task of picking fruit. "How can I help?"

He pushed the bandana tied around his forehead up higher into his receding hairline. "I've got a ladder set up for you over there."

He pointed at a nearby apple tree. "Those are the honey crisp apples. They make great cider and they're good eatin' too." He cupped his hand around his mouth and whispered, "And they make righteous hard cider, if I do say so myself."

I laughed. "Okay, Dad. I'm happy to help."

While I climbed up the ladder, he lifted a woven basket to me.

"Now, just put those in gently. You don't want to bruise them."

I squinted down at him. "But I thought these were cider apples. Why does it matter if they get bruised?"

He chuckled. "Always the logical one, aren't you? Actually, I reserve some for eating, not just for cider. We'll pick out the best lookin' apples and sell them to the local natural grocery store, Smithy's."

"Okay. I'll be extra careful then." I set about picking apples and gently placed them into the woven basket. The sun was warm on my back. I listened to the bees buzzing to and fro, collecting pollen to turn into honey for their winter reserves.

My mind wandered to pleasant thoughts of Hunter. His broad shoulders, his warm brown eyes...

"Dagnabit!" Mom screeched from the area of the garden. "Get out of my vegetables! Shoo!"

The sound of small hooves pounding the dirt path made me turn my head. A herd of goats came tearing around the corner, chasing a puff of orange fur. "Pumpkin?"

The orange ball flew out from behind a clump of bushes and headed straight toward the ladder I was standing on. Jolie, the tiny goat who served as Pumpkin's farm friend, ran ahead of the herd—likely in an attempt to protect her feline pal from the stampede.

"Pumpkin, no!" I shouted as he clambered up the ladder I was precariously balanced on.

He shot into my arms, then scaled my shoulders, his claws digging into my scalp.

The ladder wobbled as I tried to maintain my balance while trying to pull the cat from my head. Pumpkin let out a long yowl as the goats rammed the ladder.

Suddenly, Jolie, the animal whisperer, let out an ear-shattering bleat. The goats stopped mid-ram and focused their attention on her.

Sadly, the ladder had other ideas. It was in the midst of a wobble after the last goat butted it.

Like a slow-motion action scene from ninja movie, I hung in the air, cat still attached to my scalp, before we both tumbled downward.

Momentarily blacking out, I came back to consciousness flat on my back. Between the branches of the apple tree, the sky was a clear blue. My vision was not as clear. Blurry white, brown, and black shapes encircled my head like a crown.

I blinked. The blurry shapes turned into the faces of curious goats. Their strange vertical pupils made them look a little like horned demons.

"Maaaaaaa!" the littlest one said. It was Jolie. She was asking if I was all right.

"I'm fine," I croaked when the wind returned to my lungs.

"Are you?" Jonah's face hovered over the faces of the goats.

"Oh my God!" Brandi came running. "Is anything broken?"

"I have no idea." It was true. I couldn't tell if anything was broken or bruised. I was just trying to get a grip on reality.

Pumpkin rubbed up against my shoulder and walked lightly across my chest. At least my cat was okay.

"What happened?" Dad's concerned voice approached the circle of goats, with me at the center. He looked down at me. "Oh, hell."

I winced. "Is it bad? Am I broken?"

"You tell us." Jonah kneeled beside me. "Does anything hurt?"

I thought for a moment. "My head."

"Clarity! What in the world?" Mom's voice rose as she took in the scene she'd stumbled upon. She glared at the goats. "Did you kids do this?"

Jolie bleated.

"You scoundrels!" She put her hands on her hips. "First my garden, then my daughter? You ought to be ashamed of yourselves!"

"How about your neck?" Jonah asked. "Does your neck hurt? Because if it does, we shouldn't move you. You may have broken it."

Brandi kicked him. "Don't tell her she broke her neck! Are you trying to scare her to death?"

His panicked look made me giggle. "It's okay. I don't think I broke my neck." I tried sitting up, but the pain in my head made me groan.

"Let me help you." Brandi cradled my head as she helped me to sit. "You should see a doctor. You may have a concussion."

"A concussion? I can't afford to have a concussion! I'm starting a business. I have no health insurance."

"It might not be a bad one," Jonah offered. "Maybe it'll be mild, and you'll be fine in a day or two."

"I'm calling a doctor." Brandi unlocked her phone. "Wanda, which doctor do you go to?"

"We don't go to doctors," Dad said. "They're all a bunch of quacks."

"Not all of them." Mom glared at him. "The one who patched us up after Clarity's boss injured us was pretty darned good."

He shrugged. "I guess you're right. But I don't remember his name."

"Dr. Strong. And his name fits him. He's a real looker. We should find out if he's single." She winked at me.

"Mom." I groaned and tried to sit up again. "I don't need a doctor. I'm fine."

"Besides," Brandi offered, "Clarity has a thing for Zen's partner, Hunter."

Mom raised her eyebrows. "Zen won't like that."

I glared at Brandi. "You're right. He doesn't like that. And he forbade me from dating Hunter, so that's that."

"And you listened to him?" Dad said in surprise. "Since when did you do anything he told you to?"

"Yeah, yeah. I know. But I promised this time."

"You're going to let your bossy brother dictate who you do or don't fall in love with?" Dad's forehead furrowed. "That's not like you, Clarity."

I rubbed my head. "I have to respect his professional boundaries, Dad." I squinted up at him. "Are there two of you?"

Mom swatted at Dad. "Can't you see her head is hurting? We need to get her to that hot doctor."

CHAPTER 12

Twenty minutes later, I sat in the ER waiting room with Mom. The others had decided to stay at the farm to finish harvesting apples.

I held an icepack to my head and groaned. "I hope they give me something stronger than Tylenol for this headache."

A male nurse wearing blue scrubs approached us. "Clarity Bloom?" he asked.

I raised my hand. "That's me."

"I'll take you back now." He led us to a curtained-off area at the end of a row of rooms. "The doctor will be right in to see you."

"Is it Dr. Strong?" Mom asked, hope gleaming in her eyes.

The nurse nodded. "Yep. You know him?"

"He patched up my old man and me after her crazy boss tried to kill us." Mom pointed at me. "Thankfully, that creep is up for trial next week. I hope they toss him in jail and throw away the key."

Heat tinged my cheeks. "Mom."

The nurse raised his eyebrows. "Well, I'm glad Dr. Strong helped. I'll just go fetch him for you."

"Mom," I said after he was out of earshot. "You can't say stuff like that in public. It freaks people out."

She waved me away. "I can say whatever I want. If he's curious about your crazy boss, he'll ask."

I let out a heavy sigh just as the curtain parted and a very handsome man wearing a white coat came into view. He was tall, broad-shouldered, and had perfect posture. He resembled a young Paul Newman with his brilliant blue eyes and sun-kissed hair. At least, I thought he did—my vision was still a little blurry.

"Dr. Strong!" Mom rushed over to the doctor and gave him a hug. "It's so great to see you again."

The doctor smiled. "Hello, uh, I'm sorry. I don't remember your name—though I do remember you and your husband from a few weeks back." His eyes scanned her arms and face. "Looks like you've healed up nicely."

Her head bobbed up and down. "It's Wanda. Wanda Bloom. I'm all better, thanks to you, Doctor."

Ugh. Mom was making a spectacle of herself over this guy. She was practically drooling.

"Who do we have here?" He glanced at the chart in his hands. "You must be Clarity."

I stuck my hand out. "Clarity Bloom."

His smile was a brilliant white. When his hand touched mine, I felt an electric shock.

I blinked.

"Oh, sorry," he said. "Static electricity. So, it says here that you took a tumble off a ladder?"

I nodded and rubbed my head, remembering the pain.

He stepped closer. The clean scent of citrus and soap filled my nostrils.

"Does your head hurt?" His gloved fingers gently felt along my scalp. "It's swollen here." He touched a spot that made me wince. "No blood, though, except for these scratches. Looks like an animal did this?"

"That would be my cat. He climbed up me while he was escaping the goats."

Amusement shone in his eyes. He took his gloves off and set them aside. His cool fingers felt along my neck. "Does your neck hurt?"

"A little." For some reason, his gentle touch made me want to cry. I sniffled, and my eyes filled with tears.

He peered at me. "Are you sure it only hurts a little?"

"I guess it hurts more than a little." A few tears escaped and rolled down my cheeks. "I'm sorry, I don't know what's wrong with me."

"Along with pain, sadness and feeling emotional are symptoms of a concussion," he said. "I'm going to ask you a series of questions. We use a concussion assessment questionnaire to help us determine the severity."

I wiped the tears off my cheek. "Okay. Ask away."

Mom held my hand as he ran through the questions. "It'll be okay, Clarity."

That made me want to cry harder, but I bit my lip. This was so humiliating! I was crying in front of a handsome man, and I was sure I looked awful. After returning from our disastrous camping trip, I had yet to take a shower. I could almost feel the grime sticking to my skin.

When Dr. Strong finished questioning me, he scrawled something at the bottom of the page. "You've got a moderate concussion, but it's on the lower end of the scale. Almost mild, as a matter of fact. Just to be safe, I'd like to send you for a CT scan to make sure you don't have any skull fractures."

I swallowed. Skull fractures?

The male nurse came back in. "Doctor, we've got a multiple-person car accident. We need you right away."

"That's terrible." Mom stood up straighter. "Are you done with Clarity for now? Should we make an appointment for the CT scan?"

He held the curtain open. "No. We'll need to keep her here to do the scan. Normally I'd have someone come get you right away, but we're short-staffed and a big accident requires all hands on deck. Would you mind waiting for a while? Mrs. Bloom, you can have a seat in that chair and Clarity can rest where she is." He patted the bed. "I'll be back as soon as I can."

"Sure. We'll be fine here." Mom winked and sat in the chair against the wall.

The doctor let the curtain fall back into place and was gone.

Mom grinned.

"What?" I narrowed my eyes at her, but that just made my vision even more blurry.

"He likes you."

"He does not." I crossed my arms over my chest. "He's a professional. And what makes you say that?"

Her smile widened. "Because he could've had the nurse finish up here. Instead, he's making you wait so he can come back and talk some more. Maybe he'll ask you out on a date."

"No. He's making me wait because there was an accident. When that happens, he said it's all hands on deck. I'm sure that includes the nurses."

"Hmmph. You can think whatever you like, but I know love when I see it."

I groaned. "Love? He doesn't even know me. And doctors aren't supposed to flirt with patients."

"You won't be a patient for long. Once he sends you home, you'll be available for a date."

An hour later, I had trouble keeping my eyes open. I reclined on the bed and curled onto my side.

The curtain parted and Dr. Strong stepped to the side of my bed. "Sleepy?" He brushed the hair away from my face.

Mom perked up and scooted to the edge of her chair.

I paused before I turned to look at him. That seemed awfully intimate—his brushing the hair from my cheek. Maybe Mom was right...

"How are you feeling?" His voice was gentle and soothing.

"Tired and achy." I touched my head. "Can I have something for my headache, please?"

"I'm sorry." He checked my chart. "In our haste to attend to the accident patients, I neglected to give you something. My apologies."

Feeling slightly miffed and ignored, I realized if I'd been given meds, I would be feeling much better by now. I sniffled again and covered my face with my hands.

Dr. Strong patted my shoulder. "I'll send the nurse in with something, okay?"

I nodded, blinking the tears away.

He turned to Mom. "Once she's had her CT scan and is discharged, Clarity needs to go home and rest. She shouldn't drive for a few days—and no physical labor, if possible. Will you be home with her?"

I shook my head, which made it feel worse. "No! I live in Seattle. I just started a new business. I can't stay here and rest."

He gave me a stern look. "I don't think it's a good idea to go back right now. Can't you stay with your parents? I'm sure they'd love to take care of you. Isn't that right, Mrs. Bloom?"

"It's Wanda." Mom smiled sweetly. "Of course. Darren and I would love to take care of our little girl."

Dr. Strong's dazzling smile lit up the room.

The curtain parted and a frazzled-looking Zen stormed in. "Dad told us you'd rushed Clarity to the emergency room. How is she?"

The curtain opened again, and my brother's partner stepped through.

Hunter was here? He glanced at the handsome doctor hovering close to my side and the worried look he'd worn a moment before changed to something else. I rubbed my eyes to get a second look, but his expression had gone blank.

"Zen!" Mom jumped up and gave her son a big hug. "How did you know to come?"

My brother peered at me. "Clarity mentioned the murder on the rafting trip. Hunter and I have the day off, so we thought we'd go talk to Detective Reilly. We used to work together in Seattle."

"I know," I said.

"Why didn't you just call him?" Mom wanted to know.

Zen looked at Hunter and shrugged. "We haven't seen you guys in a while. Thought we'd use it as an excuse to visit. And help with the apple harvest."

Mom frowned. "But you told me before that you were working and couldn't help."

Hunter smiled. "The department just added two new detectives. They put the new guys to work on a case to break them in and gave us the day off."

"Right on. Have you boys met Dr. Strong?" She nudged Zen's arm. "He's taking excellent care of your sister."

The doctor held out his hand. "Nathan Strong. Nice to meet you."

Zen shook it. "Likewise."

Hunter shook hands too. "Hunter Ito." He glanced down at me, worry evident in his brown eyes. "Are you doing okay?"

"I'll be fine after I get something for the pain," I said with gritted teeth.

Dr. Strong opened the curtain and walked out. "Hang on. I'll get the nurse with some meds."

"Concussion?" Zen asked.

"Unfortunately, yes." My head pounded. I just wanted to pull the covers over my head and hide in the dark.

Hunter came closer and put his hand on my shoulder. "How did this happen?"

"Those rambunctious goats got into my vegetable garden. I shooed 'em out, but Pumpkin got in the middle of it all. They chased that poor little cat all the way to the ladder Clarity was standing on. And when Pumpkin dug his claws into Clarity's head, the goats rammed the ladder…" She shrugged. "Clarity fell."

Zen's gaze drifted to Hunter's hand. Hunter pulled it back and took a step back.

"Are they admitting you, then?" Zen asked.

I shrugged. "Not sure. I have to have a CT scan first to make sure my skull isn't fractured."

Hunter winced. "That doesn't sound good."

"Don't worry," Mom said. "The doctor will make sure she's all right."

"I'm sure he will," Hunter muttered under his breath.

Zen looked at me, then Hunter, and back at me. "What do you have against the doctor?"

Hunter narrowed his eyes. "He's too slick. He looks like an actor in a teeth-whitening commercial."

Zen stared at him. "So?"

Silence settled uncomfortably in the air.

Even my fuzzy brain had started to figure it out. And by the look on Zen's face, he had as well. My brother seemed both exasperated and resigned. Could he be softening the rule about his partner dating his sister?

The male nurse came in with a wheelchair. "Clarity, let's get you over to the imaging center for that scan, okay?" He helped me sit up, and he and Hunter got me into the chair.

"Are you guys staying?" I asked Zen.

He nodded. "But just until we hear the results. We'd like to talk to Detective Reilly. He's expecting us."

CHAPTER 13

When the tests came back as expected—no skull fracture, Zen and Hunter left to visit their detective friend.

Mom drove me home, chatting the entire way back.

"I didn't see a ring on Dr. Strong's finger." She glanced at me.

"Uh huh." I stared out the window and breathed a sigh of relief when we turned down the long gravel road to their house.

Mom parked the car and stared at me. "Clarity, why don't you ask that nice doctor out? It's not the 1950s anymore. He'll be flattered you asked him."

My head still hurt, and I wasn't in the mood to talk about this with her. "Dating is not on my mind right now. I just want to lie down."

"All right. I get it. Stay right there. I'll open the car door for you."

Before she could come around to my side, Jonah and Brandi came running.

"Clarity, are you all right?" Brandi yanked the door open. "Oh, God. You look bad."

"Thanks," I grumbled.

"Brandi, really?" Jonah helped me out of the car. "She looks good for having fallen out of a tree."

"You're not making this any better," I told him.

"I mean, you always look beautiful—no matter what." He put his arm around me and led me to the bed and breakfast door.

"Nice save," I groaned.

Once inside, I lowered myself onto the couch. Mom fussed with the pillows and made sure I was comfortable.

"I'll go whip up some refreshments. How do some nice wheatgrass smoothies sound?"

"Uh, no thanks, Mom. But iced tea sounds good if you have it." If I had to drink another one of her wheatgrass smoothies, I was going to admit myself back into the hospital. Even cafeteria food was better than some of the stuff she "whipped up."

"Right on, sunshine. I'll get you some iced tea." She turned to look at my friends. "How about you two?"

"Iced tea would be fine." Jonah sat down next to me.

"For me, too." Brandi took a step toward the front door. "I'll help you carry it over."

Jonah leaned back and against the couch cushions. He put his hands behind his head and propped his feet up on the coffee table. "What a day."

I winced. "I know. I'm sorry."

"It's not your fault. You didn't prompt those goats to charge. And you didn't kill Ray's cousin either. It was all bad luck."

The last thing I wanted to think about was murder. "The goats didn't mean anything by it. They just wanted to play with Pumpkin, I guess."

The door opened. Mom and Brandi came in carrying glasses of iced tea, each with a wedge of lemon stuck on the rim. Pumpkin wandered into the room and hopped on my lap, purring.

"Hello, baby." I scratched him behind his ears. "Have you gotten over the goat debacle already?"

As if on cue, Jolie appeared in the doorway. "Maaaa."

Pumpkin jumped off my lap and greeted his friend by rubbing his cheek on her shoulder.

"Your cat sure loves Jolie." Mom scratched her goat behind the ears. "If you want to leave him here with us, that's fine by me. Jolie digs him."

The thought of giving up Pumpkin brought instant tears to my eyes. "I can't give him up. I'd be so lonely without him."

Mom cocked her head to one side. "Well, you could move in with us. Pumpkin could be with his farm friends all the time. He loves it here. And you could see that nice doctor more often."

I wiped my eyes. Pumpkin was starved for companionship. I felt awful. Had I been selfish to deny him a friend and leaving him alone all day while I went off to work? But moving away from Seattle and leaving my new business and my friends behind was not an option. Oh, God. And moving in with Mom and Dad? No way.

"I'm not interested in the doctor, Mom. And I can't close my business—I just started it."

"You could relocate your business here!"

I shook my head. "There's not enough crime here to keep a private detective business going."

"But there was a murder." Mom raised her eyebrows. "Isn't that enough?"

"Mom..."

"Anyone home?" Zen's voice called from the front yard.

"In here, honey!" Mom answered.

Zen and Hunter appeared in the doorway.

"How are you feeling, sis?" my brother asked.

I shrugged. "Okay, I guess." The truth was, I was feeling blue about everything. This wasn't like me—I wasn't the emotional type. And realizing that made me feel even worse. I burst into tears.

Hunter nudged Jonah over and sat beside me. The look of concern on his face made me cry harder. "Is your head still hurting?"

"No," I blubbered. "It's not that. Mom wants me to give up my business and," I half snorted, half choked out, "she wants me to move back home with them!"

A blob of snot flew out of my nose and landed on Hunter's pant leg. He struggled to keep his expression neutral.

Horror burned my insides.

Brandi instantly appeared, tissue in hand. She dabbed at the gelatinous goo and whisked it away as quickly as it had appeared.

I gave her a grateful smile, even though my embarrassment was still cartwheeling in my stomach. "Thank you, Brandi." I turned to Hunter. "I'm sorry about that."

"No problem. I've had worse things stain my pants."

Now it was his turn to turn red. "That came out wrong. I meant that, as a cop, I've had stuff get on my clothing. Like blood, guts, vomit, you name it."

Zen burst into laughter. "This is the most entertainment I've had all week." Then his face fell, and his smile faded. He didn't want us to be entertaining. He wanted us to be apart.

I glared at my brother.

Hunter glared at his partner.

Brandi and Jonah exchanged amused but nervous smiles.

"Well," Mom said stiffly, breaking the awkward moment, "the offer is always open, Clarity. You're always welcome to move home—or not."

I could tell that I'd hurt her feelings, but I was not in the position to fix it. My head still hurt, and I was still feeling down. The snot hadn't helped.

"Hello?" A man's voice called from the driveway. "Anybody home?"

"In here!" Mom yelled.

A middle-aged man wearing faded jeans and a flannel shirt appeared in the doorway. "Hey, Wanda."

"Hey, Louie." Mom went to hug him. She introduced him to all of us, then asked, "What brings you out here?"

"I owe you some money, remember?" His expression was sheepish as he shifted his weight from one foot to the other.

"I was wondering when you were going to pay us back." Mom crossed her arms and gave him the look she always gave us when we hadn't done our chores.

"The thing is…" Louie looked down at his feet. "The weed you sold me was super awesome, and you were generous to let me start a tab. But I shouldn't have kept coming back for more. That was irresponsible of me."

Zen cringed.

Hunter bit his lip to keep from laughing.

"And you don't have the cash to pay me yet, right?" Mom tapped her foot. "You're going to have to come up with something, Louie. Or else, we'll have to take something of yours in exchange."

He'd likely been waiting for her to bring this up because his smile was too quick to appear. "See, that's why I'm here. I have something for you. It's not cash, but you could sell them for cash. 'Cause they're pretty valuable items. In fact, they're worth a lot more than I owe you."

Mom's brows furrowed. "What are the items?"

"Come take a look. I have them in the truck."

Hunter whispered in my ear. "This, I've got to see. Want me to help you outside?"

My head hurt, but my curiosity won out over the pain. "I'm in," said. "Help me up."

With Hunter's arm around me waist, we followed Louie to the driveway. The old beat-up Ford truck was parked haphazardly, two wheels in the grass and two on the dirt. Behind the smudged glass windshield, I spied the tops of two fuzzy heads. Were those children? Was he giving Mom his children in exchange for a marijuana debt?

Louie opened the passenger door and bowed with a flourish. "Let me introduce you to the last two pups of Daisy's litter. I haven't named them yet—that's for you to decide."

Mom stood, open-mouthed. "You brought us puppies instead of dough?"

Louie grinned. "Aren't they great?"

Mom frowned. "Louie, take a look around. Does it look like I have a shortage of animals?"

Louie's head moved from side to side as he surveyed the farm. Goats were milling about, trying not to step on the chickens who were busy pecking at insects in the dirt. Pumpkin and Jolie sauntered out of the bed and breakfast and to see what all the fuss was about.

"Well, no." He pointed to the two pups, wiggling and wagging their tails on the bench seat of the truck. "But these are AKC registered golden retrievers. They're worth at least one thousand dollars each."

Mom put her hands on her hips. "Then why aren't you selling them and giving me the cash?"

Louie swiped the sweat off his forehead. "Uh, actually. Me and Daisy are headed out of town. We sold the other six puppies, but it wasn't enough to keep my little house from getting foreclosed on. The sheriff's coming by in an hour to make sure I'm gone."

"Why is the sheriff getting involved?" Mom asked.

"I'm way behind on the mortgage. The bank's takin' my house back. The sheriff's just there to make sure I vacate the premises."

Mom made a tsk-tsk noise. "That's too bad, Louie. I'm sorry that happened to you. Maybe you should stop smoking so much dope. That stuff depletes your energy. You should drink wheatgrass smoothies instead. They clear your mind and give you lots of pep. Want one for the road?"

Louie looked slightly horrified, but I could tell he didn't want to hurt my mom's feelings. "Yeah, okay. That's nice of you."

"I'll whip one up in a jiffy. Be right back." Mom hurried to the main house and closed the door behind her.

Louie reached into the truck and pulled out the first dog, a reddish-gold pup.

"Ooooh!" Brandi squealed and rushed to take it from Louie's hands. "This is the cutest puppy I've ever seen." She peeked under the puppy. "It's a boy!"

Mom came out with a glass mason jar filled with bright green liquid. "Here you go, Louie. I'd give you a straw for the road, but straws are terrible for the environment. You can sip it just fine without one."

Louie sniffed the concoction and tried not to make a face. "Thank you, Wanda. Much appreciated." He set the jar in one of the truck's cup holders and then picked up the other pup, still wiggling on the seat.

He handed the second cream-colored pup to me. Its dark brown eyes and nose were a striking contrast against its light coat.

"This one's a male too," Louie said.

The puppy's tail wagged furiously, and he stretched to lick my face.

My heart melted, and I momentarily forgot about my headache. "Aw! What a sweet boy."

Pumpkin, who'd been sitting next to my feet, sat up on his hind legs and put his front paws on my knees.

"You want to meet the puppy?" I knelt down and let Pumpkin sniff him. I put the pup down on the ground and Pumpkin purred as he rubbed his cheek on the puppy's side.

"Well, if that's not the cutest thing I've ever seen!" Mom grinned. "Pumpkin likes goats and dogs. That's an unusual cat you've got there."

Louie interrupted the adorable scene between cat and dog. "What do you think, Wanda? Is it a deal?"

Mom sighed. "It's a deal. You mentioned that you don't have a house to go home to. Where will you go?"

"My sister in Oregon said we can come live with her until I get back on my feet. I have a storage trailer back home—I mean, back at my old place. I'm headed there to pick up Daisy and my stuff before I hit the road."

Mom gave him a quick hug. "Well, then. You take care. Good luck on your new adventure." She pointed at him. "And stay away from Mary Jane. She'll make you fat and lazy, if you know what I mean."

Brandi wrinkled her nose. "Who is Mary Jane?"

Zen shook his head. "Good grief."

"It's slang for weed," I whispered. I wondered why Mom seemed so against it, considering she'd grown and sold weed for a while. I guessed she and Dad did what they had to do to get by.

Dad came out of the barn. "Hey, Louie!" he called. "What you up to?"

"Just stopped by to pay a debt and to say goodbye!" Louie waved and climbed into his truck. "Take care of the pups. They were Daisy's last litter."

His eyes misted over as he took one last look at the dogs. "Oh! I almost forgot!" He rolled down the window and handed a folder and a half-empty bag of dog food to Mom. "Their papers are all in there, including their vaccination records and stuff. They're eight weeks old today."

"Right on." Mom waved.

Louie backed up his truck and turned toward the highway, dust kicking up behind the tires.

"Well, that was a bust." Mom pursed her lips. "I guess I could try to sell these little guys." She patted the red pup on the head. "Sure are cute, though."

"What've we got here?" Dad looked from one dog to the others. "Louie brought us dogs? What for?"

"As payment for the money he owed us for the pot." Mom shook her head. "I didn't really think he would pay us back anyhow."

"Huh." Dad shrugged and glanced at me. "I thought you were supposed to rest."

I picked up the cream-colored puppy. "Yeah, I will. I'm going to bring this little guy with me, if that's okay with you."

"Sure. Why not?" Dad started back to the barn. "Say, why don't you rest on the patio? I just built a nice little sitting area behind the B&B. It's got comfortable lounge furniture and everything. There's even a barbecue pit back there."

I relaxed. Sitting outdoors in the sun and fresh air sounded lovely. "Yeah. Sounds great, Dad. Thanks."

✳✳✳

The patio was as promised. Dad had created a spectacular stone tile patio. A colorful awning stretched out from the back wall of the B&B and provided some welcome shade.

I sat on the cushy couch and put the puppy on my lap. Pumpkin hopped up beside me and cuddled up next to the pup.

"He seems to like you and Pumpkin," Zen said.

The little dog yawned and leaned into Pumpkin's soft fur.

The red-gold puppy yipped to join the party. Jonah lifted him up and plunked him down beside me.

"This is the best medicine ever." I let the warmth of the animals settle over me.

"Is your head feeling any better?" Hunter sat in the chair next to the couch. He reached over and brushed the hair off my shoulder.

Zen coughed.

"A little." Now that I was feeling better, I was more aware of the tension between Zen and Hunter. I wished my brother would just lay off us for a while. His chaperone routine was really starting to get on my nerves.

"What did you find out about the murder?" I stroked the sleeping dog on my lap.

"Not a lot," Zen said. "But it's very likely that someone in your rafting party did it.

Jonah frowned. "We kind of figured that, but it's still hard to believe."

"Who would do such a thing?" Brandi asked. "To hit someone over the head with an oar? That's just awful."

"The most likely suspect would be someone who hated Arnold." Hunter glanced at Zen.

My brother cleared his throat. "From what Detective Reilly said, it seems as though Ray and Arnold had a rocky relationship."

"Are you saying what I think you're saying?" Brandi's eyes flashed. "Ray wouldn't hurt a fly."

"How do you know that?" Zen asked. "Didn't you say you met him a few days ago?"

Brandi bristled and got to her feet. "Yeah? Well, in that short time, I've learned that he is the kindest, most amazing man I have ever met."

"Hey, hey," Hunter said. "Calm down. No one is accusing Ray of anything. They're still sifting through all the evidence. Nothing definitive has come out of the interviews. Let's just see what happens, okay?"

She glowered at him. "Nothing will come out of the interviews because he's innocent."

He nodded. "Good. Then you have nothing to worry about."

CHAPTER 14

We were all gathered in Mom and Dad's kitchen, dishing up plates of hummus and fresh vegetables from the garden.

The kitchen was a mish-mash of styles. The walls were painted a sunshine yellow. The vinyl floor was an unfortunate shade of avocado green. But the appliances were stainless steel and somewhat new.

"I insist you stay the night." Mom put her hands on her hips. "You boys don't need to drive back to Seattle in the dark."

"I don't know, Mom," Zen said. "We should get back to work."

Hunter took a piece of pita bread off a platter. "It's pretty unlikely they'll need us tomorrow. Plus, we already let the captain know we were helping the police here. He was glad to use this as an interdepartmental case study. Apparently, they're looking to do more of this kind of thing in the future. Makes him look good."

Zen groaned. "All right. We'll stay. But just for one night."

Mom grinned. "Right on. There are two empty rooms in the bed and breakfast. You can make yourselves comfortable."

Inside, my heart was doing a happy dance. Even though my head hurt, I was thrilled that Hunter would be in near proximity to me. I felt better just thinking about it.

I put my plate on the table with a glass of water and collapsed into a chair.

Hunter slid into one next to me and laid his hand lightly on my shoulder. "Doing okay?"

My heart needed to stop galloping. Was I sacrificing my health by sitting beside him? "Yeah, my head doesn't hurt as much."

Zen took a seat across from Hunter and gave me a stony glare. "I'll take the room next to yours, Clarity."

Hunter frowned.

Why was Zen being such an ass? I turned to Hunter. "Thank you for being concerned for my well-being. I appreciate that you care."

I shot an angry look at Zen and took a bite of a carrot, the crunching sound punctuating my words. "Unlike my brother. By the way, the only available rooms are upstairs. Brandi and I have bedrooms downstairs, for your information."

The others joined us at the table and almost immediately picked up on the tension.

"So." Brandi cleared her throat. "Are you going to see Detective Reilly tomorrow?"

"Yep." Hunter rushed to answer her. "First thing in the morning."

"Will you be able to share what you know with us?" Jonah asked.

"Normally, I'd say no. But since we're not officially assigned to this case, I think we can share some details." Hunter sipped his water.

"But nothing that would compromise the investigation," my brother said. His phone buzzed. "Excuse me. I have to take this." He got up and motioned for Hunter to join him before heading through the open door to the backyard.

"What's that all about?" Brandi craned her neck to see where they'd gone.

"Police business." Mom brushed a strand of graying hair away from her face. "They're a secretive bunch."

Brandi shrugged. "Maybe they have some news about the murder."

"I hope they solve it quickly," Jonah said. "It will be nice to have things go back to normal." He glanced at Brandi.

"Yeah." She pushed a carrot stick into her hummus and drew a heart shape. "I just want things to be okay for Ray."

The back door was open, and a light breeze wafted in, carrying the scent of lavender, hay, and goat.

Jolie appeared in the doorway. Pumpkin and the two puppies were following her as if she were a mama duck and they were her ducklings.

"Maaa," she said.

"Thanks for bringing them back, Jolie. I better get you little dudes some dinner." Mom got up and dished up a bowl of cat crunchies, two bowls of puppy kibble, and a bowl of vegetables and hummus for Jolie. She set them down in front of the animals and they dug in.

Zen came back inside.

"What's up?" Hunter asked.

"That was Reilly." Zen joined us at the table. "Cause of death is as expected. Blunt force trauma to the back of the head.

Forensics is still working on discovering evidence—fibers, blood, etc."

Brandi put down her fork. "Did they mention anything about who the suspects are?"

Zen paused. "Everyone on the rafting trip is a suspect."

"Including us?" Jonah asked.

"Well, some are more likely suspects than others. But, yes. Everyone is a suspect for now."

"What about Ray? Is he okay? I've been texting him all day, and he hasn't responded." Brandi looked hopeful.

"The police have asked him to stay in town." Zen glanced at Hunter.

"That's weird." Brandi frowned. "The police never asked us to stay in town."

I felt a pang of empathy for my friend. Whatever was going on with Ray was not good. The fact that he was avoiding her made it worse. "He's probably with his family. I imagine he's helping with funeral plans. They must be devastated."

"You're right." She sighed. "I'm probably the last thing on his mind right now."

"I didn't mean it that way." God, I was making it worse for her. "I'm sure you're important to him. It's just that he's probably dealing with a lot right now."

"It's all right," Brandi said. "I know. I just…"

"I'm sure everything will be okay," Jonah said. "Brandi, when we're done eating, how about you help me get some more apples picked. There's still quite a bit more to do."

"Good idea." Zen seemed grateful for the subject changed. "Clarity, you can take care of the puppies while the rest of us finish with the harvest."

"Yeah, okay." Secretly, I was glad to have some time to rest without having to think about Arnold's murder.

✳✳✳

The puppies were a handful.

After wriggling around and biting each other's faces for a few minutes, they soon tired of it and attacked me instead.

"Ouch! That's my toe!" I pulled the reddish puppy off my foot. The cream-colored one took its place and sank its little shark teeth into my soft flesh. So much for resting.

Mom poked her head through the open door. "Are you okay? I heard you shout."

I sighed. "These little rascals think I'm a teething toy."

She came inside and put her hands on her hips. "You were supposed to let her rest, you little demons."

The puppies discovered a new victim and went after Mom's feet.

I stifled a laugh as she tried shaking them off her leg.

"Mom, what are you going to name them?" I asked. "You can't call them 'little demons' forever, you know."

"Well, Louie said he already registered them with the AKC. That means they might already have names." She reached for the papers Louie had handed her before he left. "It says here that the red one is called Skagit's Comet Shooting Star—I guess Comet for short." She ruffled his ears as he pulled at her pantleg. "And the light one is called Skagit's Kodiak Big Dipper. Kodiak for short."

"That's cute," I said. "You should keep those names."

Mom frowned. "See, that's the thing. I don't think I want to keep the pups."

I sat up straighter. "What?"

Hunter wandered into the house. "Just checking to see if you needed anything."

"No, I'm fine. Mom was just telling me she doesn't plan to keep the puppies."

Hunter glanced at the pups, back to wrestling on the floor near my mom's feet. "Why not?"

"Dad and I have too much to do already," she said. "Pups like these need to be properly trained and given lots of attention."

My heart fluttered, and I almost started crying again. "This is terrible news. I was looking forward to seeing them grow up."

Mom's eyes twinkled. "If you want them, they're yours."

For once, I was speechless.

There was a long pause before she spoke again. "Pumpkin needs animal friends, Clarity. And since I don't think you can have goats in your neighborhood, why not take the puppies?"

I pictured my life with Pumpkin and added two puppies. Two? "Mom, I don't know if I can take care of both pups. That's a lot of work."

Mom turned to Hunter. "How about you take one and Clarity takes the other one?"

Hunter froze. "Me?"

"The red one—Comet. He seems to like you." Mom pointed to the red fluff ball who had begun tugging on Hunter's shoelace.

"But I work a lot of hours," Hunter said. "And I have an unpredictable schedule."

I sat up straighter. "I can watch him when you're at work. That way, Pumpkin and Kodiak will have friends to play with."

"But you work a lot, too." Hunter frowned.

My spirits suddenly lifted, and my head felt better. "I have my own business. I can bring them to work with me. And I can work from home whenever I want, unless I have meetings scheduled." My heart did a little dance. I could see Hunter more often if I took care of his puppy.

Mom slapped her leg. "Right on. It's settled, then."

CHAPTER 15

"Go fish!" Mom cackled.

Hunter, Dad, Mom, and me were lounging on the two couches playing a lengthy card game when a knock at the front door startled us.

"Come in!" Mom yelled.

"Did someone send for a doctor?" Dr. Strong entered the living room carrying a beautiful bouquet of summer flowers. "How's the patient?"

Mom practically swooned. "Look, Clarity, the doctor brought you flowers. How thoughtful. I'll just put these in water before they wilt." She took the flowers from him and went into the kitchen to find a vase.

The doctor was wearing a light blue shirt that accentuated his bright blue eyes, and beige linen pants. He looked like someone who'd just breezed in from a beach vacation. His blond hair and tan contributed to the surfer boy, cover model look.

He sat down next to me on the couch and laid a cool hand on my forehead. "How are you feeling?"

"Surprisingly well, thank you." I realized that I did feel well. I wasn't sleepy, weepy, or dopey like before. I smiled. Those descriptions made me sound like one of the seven dwarfs.

"Glad to hear that." His white grin nearly blinded me. "Do you still have a headache?"

I shook my head. "It's mostly gone."

"How about dizziness?"

"I haven't stood up for a while. Let me see." I got up from the couch and stood for a moment before sitting back down. "Nope. Not dizzy."

"Fantastic. A mild to moderate concussion usually takes seven to ten days to recover from—sometimes longer. When you go home, I'd like you to check in with your regular doctor. We can transfer your chart to them. I think I can officially pronounce that you're no longer my patient."

Out of the corner of my eye, I saw Hunter bristle. He walked around the couch and sat next to me. Now I had two hot guys sitting on either side.

Dr. Strong smiled at Hunter. "You were at the hospital when Clarity was there. You're Clarity's brother? The detective, right?"

I cringed. This was awkward.

"No. I'm not her brother. But I am a detective. Her brother is my partner." Hunter said. His posture was rigid.

Zen, Brandi, and Jonah walked in through the open back door, laughing about something the goats did.

"Did you see how Jolie put that billy goat in his place?" Brandi giggled. "I get a real kick out of that girl."

Brandi and Jonah looked at the two men on either side of me and stared. Jonah raised an eyebrow.

Zen stopped when he saw both Hunter and the doctor staring each other down. "Dr. Strong. What happened? Is Clarity going back to the hospital?"

Brandi and Jonah exchanged a confused look. They hadn't come to the hospital with me and didn't know anything about Dr. Strong.

The doctor stood up. "No, no. She's fine. In fact, I think after she gets a little rest, she can go home anytime. Speaking of rest and relaxation," he said turning to me, "I have tickets to Shakespeare in the park. No loud music—because you don't want that if you still have symptoms of a concussion. I hope you don't think I'm being forward, but I have a picnic basket in the car and a blanket to lay out on the grass. You can just relax. What do you say?"

Hunter started to say something. But Mom had come in carrying the vase filled with flowers. She'd heard the date proposal. "Oh, hon, you should go. Have a great time. And we can rest easy knowing that there's a doctor with you in case anything happens."

"But—" Hunter said.

"You should go, Clarity," Zen interrupted. "You deserve a nice night out."

Hunter's jaw tightened, and he closed his eyes for a moment.

I was torn. Hunter was upset. The puppies were snuggled next to my feet, all cozy and warm. But Mom and Zen wanted me to go. I looked over to see Brandi and Jonah's reaction. They looked as helpless as I felt.

"Go on," Mom said. "I insist that you go." I could hear the desperation in her voice. Mom wanted a grandchild. Her nine children seemed averse to becoming parents, me included. I was sure she thought the doctor and me could pop out a grandchild or two. But we had to go out on a date first.

Dr. Strong's brilliant smile lit up his handsome face. He held his hand out to me. "What do you think?"

I took in a deep breath and let it out slowly. I looked at Zen. He seemed like he wanted to push me into the arms of the doctor. I knew it was all about him trying to keep me away from his partner. And I'd promised him I would stay away from Hunter. "Okay. I'll go."

Hunter deflated like a balloon with an air leak.

My heart sank. I wanted to go to Shakespeare in the park with Hunter. I didn't know Dr. Strong. I didn't even remember his first name.

"Good." The doctor stood up and helped me to my feet. "Bring a light jacket. It gets a little chilly in the evening."

***

Twenty minutes later, we arrived at the park. Dr. Strong came around to my side of the Porsche and opened the door.

He reached in and helped me out. "Stay right there. I'll get the picnic basket and blanket."

I watched him unload the car. An eagle flew overhead, calling to its mate somewhere in the tall fir trees nearby.

The parking lot was filling up with cars, everyone getting out and chattering as they carried baskets of food, blankets, and camping chairs to the low, grassy hill overlooking the outdoor stage.

"Ready?" He had a blanket over one shoulder and carried a basket in one hand.

"Sure. Can I carry something?"

"Oh, no, no. No lifting heavy things or doing anything too strenuous," he said.

I hated to admit it, but I felt kind of pampered and special. Maybe this wasn't such a bad idea after all. Still, I felt bad about Hunter. I could tell how upset he'd been when Dr. Strong appeared at the door. If Zen wasn't being so hard-nosed about the whole partner dating thing…

A large yellow butterfly fluttered ahead, showing us the way to the park.

The line to get in moved quickly and we found a relatively flat spot to spread out the blanket. Dr. Strong helped me get settled and we sat, watching people find places to sit.

"I'm so glad you could join me," he said.

"Me too," I responded automatically, before I could determine if that was true or not.

I felt his eyes on me, and I knew he wanted to engage in conversation. I forced myself to say something—anything to break the air of awkwardness.

"Um, so… Dr. Strong, how long have you lived here?" I fiddled with my shoelace.

"It's Nathan." He smiled. "And I moved here just a few months ago from California."

His teeth were so white. How did anyone have teeth that white?

"California," I said. "It's nice there. What part?"

"Los Angeles. How about you, Clarity? How long have you lived here?"

"I grew up all over the Puget Sound area. Mom and Dad moved us around a lot. I live in Seattle now."

"Seattle's a nice city." He opened the picnic basket and lifted out a container of blueberries, a package of crackers, and a wheel of brie. "Care for an appetizer? I also have a delicious pasta salad, fried chicken, and chocolate cake for dessert."

Now he was getting my attention. My stomach rumbled. but I also had questions. "That looks fabulous."

He handed me a plate and a plastic fork. "But how did you know I would be feeling well enough to attend the show?"

"I guess you could call me an eternal optimist." He laughed. "And I knew your concussion was somewhat mild. I was hoping you felt the same spark I did when we met at the hospital."

I studied him. He seemed sincere. But how could he feel a spark for a person he'd just met—and who'd arrived at the hospital disheveled after a weird goat accident? It wasn't like I was all dressed up and prettified for this date either.

"The moment I saw those bright blue eyes." He stroked my cheek with his thumb. "And that raven hair, I was smitten."

What in the world? I leaned back to avoid being touched. I had just met this guy. He seemed to be coming on awfully strong.

"I'd love to try the fried chicken," I said, changing the subject.

He seemed to snap out of his attempt to win me over. "Sure." He pulled out a foil pan and opened it. The heavenly smell made me salivate like Pavlov's dog. I licked my lips in anticipation.

Nathan put the chicken on a paper plate and added a scoop of pasta salad. "Save some room for the chocolate cake. It's to die for." He handed me a fork and a napkin. "I brought sparkling apple cider since you should probably stay away from alcohol for a few days."

My goodness. Either he was incredibly thoughtful, or he was the ultimate player. Seemed like he had this whole thing down.

Just then, a couple walked past us to a section a few rows below. Was that Astrid from our rafting trip? I sat up straight and craned my neck to get a better look.

The statuesque blonde was wearing a Mediterranean blue maxi dress with a slit up the side exposing her tan, muscled legs. It was her. I was sure of it.

Instead of the braids I'd normally seen her wear, her hair was free and straight, looking like she'd had a professional Brazilian blow dry. She looked the love child of Christy Brinkley and Heidi Klum. Or a Nordic princess on a beach holiday.

My head turned to see if Dr. Strong had noticed what I was looking at. He had.

"Do you know that woman?" he asked.

"Yes. Sort of. She was on the river rafting trip I was on over the weekend."

His lips twitched in amusement. "River rafting! See now, I would've thought you'd been in more danger on a rafting trip than at home with your parents."

I laughed. "Oh, all kinds of things happen on a farm. Especially with goats in the mix."

He shrugged. "I wouldn't know anything about goats, being a city boy."

My attention wandered back to Astrid. Who was that man she was with? It looked like—

"Clarity? Are you all right? You aren't getting lightheaded, are you?" Nathan's look of concern brought me back to our date.

A date. Was I really on a date? The thought suddenly struck me. I mean, I knew that's what this was, but somehow, it seemed completely bizarre. I liked Hunter. He liked me. Zen made me promise I wouldn't date his partner. And now, here I was on a date with a handsome doctor. In the park. About to watch a Shakespeare play.

I came back to reality. "Oh, I'm fine. I'm just trying to figure out who the man with Astrid is."

I sat up on my knees and strained to see him. There were several people blocking my field of vision. Then, I saw him. It was Carlson! The venture capitalist from our rafting trip. And his wife was nowhere to be seen.

"Are they married?" Nathan asked.

"No. That's the thing. He's married to someone else. And she was interested in my friend's boyfriend, not Carlson. I'm so confused."

He looked down at the picnic basket. "People are strange. How about some sparkling apple cider?"

"I'd love some. Thank you." I took the cup and sipped. "This is really good."

"One of my patients dropped this by after I popped his dislocated shoulder back into place."

I winced. "Ouch. I guess I got off lucky just having a mild concussion."

"Ladies and gentlemen!" A voice crackled over the microphone. "Welcome to the Shakespeare in the Park performance of The Taming of the Shrew. It's our last show of the summer. If you like the show, there's a donation box at the ticket table, or if you'd like to make an online donation instead, you can go to our website. Please turn off your cell phones and enjoy the show!"

The opening scene began, but I couldn't take my eyes off Astrid and Carlson. He kept inching closer to Astrid, but it seemed as though his advances were unwanted. Carlson wrapped his arm around her shoulder, and she shook it off. What was going on?

If Astrid wasn't interested in Carlson, why was she here with him?

As the sun dropped a little lower in the sky, the lights on stage grew brighter. A mosquito buzzed by my ear. Oh, great. Those buggers loved me.

Nathan watched me slap at the little vampire and said, "Here." He handed me a small spray bottle of bug spray. "This stuff works great."

"Thanks," I whispered and proceeded to spray myself from head to toe. "You've thought of everything."

He smiled, his eyes even bluer in the dim light. "Careful. That's DEET—highly toxic."

I coughed. "Now you tell me. Well, at least I'll die without being itchy."

Nathan laughed and scooted closer. "You've got quite the sense of humor, Miss Bloom."

"I try."

"Shhh." The woman in front of me turned and put her finger to her lips.

"Sorry," I whispered. I tried focusing on what the actors were saying. But it was Shakespeare. You had to pay full attention if you wanted to understand what was going on. I was lost.

My eyes wandered to Astrid and Carlson. Something was going on between the two of them. There were angry whispers. Her cheeks went from tan to red, and suddenly, she reached out and slapped Carlson across the face.

The shusher in front of me sucked in a breath. "What is wrong with these people? This is not the way to behave during a performance."

Though I hated people who policed everyone else, I had to agree. It was bad enough that Nathan and I were talking—but even worse that Astrid had clobbered Carlson—though I could hardly blame her. That guy was a creep.

Astrid grabbed her purse and stormed away while Carlson rubbed his cheek.

"Wow." Nathan watched her disappear over the hill. "That was unexpected."

"Yeah." I pretended to pay attention to the stage, but instead, I wondered if what I'd just witnessed had anything to do with Arnold's murder.

CHAPTER 16

"Thank you for a lovely evening." I pulled my jacket tighter around me. Nathan and I were standing on the front steps of my parents' bed and breakfast wing.

"Thanks for feeling well enough to come along. I had a great time." He looked down at his shoes and shuffled his feet before looking back up. "Would you like to go out again sometime?"

I was afraid of this. Nathan was a nice man, and he seemed to genuinely like me. My heart, though, was somewhere else. Besides, the doctor was crossing boundaries I felt he shouldn't cross. I wasn't entirely comfortable with him asking me out while I was sort of his patient.

"Maybe—I'm not sure when we're heading back to Seattle," I said, knowing that I didn't want to continue this.

"I'll take that maybe as a yes." His smile was dazzling in the darkness. He bent down and kissed my cheek. "Good night, Clarity. I'll call you tomorrow."

Damn. I should've just said no. "Good night." I opened the door of the bed and breakfast and let myself in.

Zen, Hunter, Brandi, and Jonah were watching the latest true crime series on the big screen. Beer bottles and pizza boxes were strewn on the coffee table.

When I entered, all heads swiveled. Hunter sat up straight, his brow furrowed. Zen used the remote to pause the show and looked hopeful. Brandi and Jonah still seemed as confused as they had earlier when the doctor had asked me out.

"How was your date?" Zen asked.

I shrugged. "It was all right, I guess."

Hunter scooted over and made a space for me on the couch.

Zen cleared his throat. "Clarity, don't feel like you have to talk about your date. Some things are better kept to oneself."

I frowned. "It's all right. I don't mind talking about it. Nathan is a nice person. I guess I'm just not feeling it. Maybe it's because of my concussion. Or maybe it's because of other reasons." I glanced at Hunter.

"Was the play good?" Brandi asked.

I scratched my head. "I wasn't paying attention, so I don't know if it was good or bad."

Hunter shifted on the couch. I could feel the tension through the cushions.

Jonah leaned forward. "Because you were really into the good doctor instead of the show?"

Realizing how that must've come across, my cheeks flushed. "No! Absolutely not. Get your mind out of the gutter."

"So, why weren't you paying attention? Did your head hurt?" Brandi asked.

"No. My head is much better. What distracted me was that I saw Astrid in the audience."

"The same Astrid from our rafting trip?" Jonah asked.

"Yep. She was with a guy. Want to take a guess as to who it was?"

Brandi frowned and put her hand over her heart. "It wasn't Ray, was it?"

"Of course not! Ray is better than that. She was with Carlson."

"Carlson?" Brandi said. "But he's married!"

"Exactly. I couldn't take my eyes off them."

The tiniest twitch of Hunter's lips seemed to indicate he was amused.

"Wait a minute," Jonah said. "What was Dr. Strong doing during this whole scenario?"

"Huh? What do you mean?"

"I mean, if you were glued to the two adulterers, what was your date doing?" He shrugged. "Just curious."

"I don't know." I fidgeted with my hair. "He asked who the people were, but he kept trying to give me food. And honestly, he was being way too friendly for a guy on a first date with a woman he barely knows."

Zen seemed startled and leaned forward.

Hunter frowned. "Did he try anything?"

"Not really. Just kind of invading my personal space. He kissed me at the front door."

"What?" Hunter stood up.

"But just on the cheek."

"Oh." He sat back down.

"Excuse me for a second. I need to go check on something." Zen got up and headed for the front door.

"Do you need my help?" Hunter asked.

"No. I got it." Zen left.

"Well, anyway," I said. "I'm glad to be back here with you guys." I looked around the room. "Where's Pumpkin?"

"He's in the main house with the puppies. They were all snuggled together, sleeping. We didn't want to wake them." Brandi smiled. "Pumpkin is going to love having them around all the time."

"So am I."

Brandi's phone buzzed. She glanced at the screen. "It's a text from Ray!"

"What did he say?" I asked.

She took a moment to read, then said, "He's sorry he hasn't texted me. His family lives here in the valley, and they're trying to deal with Arnold's death. His aunt and uncle are devastated. Arnold is their only son. He says the funeral is tomorrow and is hoping we can all attend."

I leaned back. "Wow. How awful. Poor Ray."

"Yeah." Brandi sighed. She looked back down at her screen. "The service is at two o'clock at the Skagit Valley Funeral Home."

Jonah paled. "I didn't bring anything to wear to a funeral. All I have are cargo shorts, camping shirts, and the khaki slacks I wore last night."

Brandi looked as worried as Jonah did. "I don't think any of us brought somber clothing we could wear to funeral."

"I can safely say that neither my mom or dad will have anything we can borrow. They mostly wear tie dye t-shirts and jeans. That means that we'll be going on a quick trip to the mall tomorrow morning." I got up from the couch and started stacking pizza boxes under my arm.

"Wait a second. You should rest." Hunter took the boxes away from me. "I'll take these and the beer bottles out to the compost and recycling bins."

"Thanks."

Brandi watched him leave. "What is up with that date? Why did your doctor ask you out? You were just released from the hospital."

Jonah crossed his arms. "I was wondering the same thing. I know you're not his regular patient anymore, but it seems a little creepy that he'd ask you out."

I looked down at my hands. "I know. I probably shouldn't have gone with him. But Mom was pressuring me, and I didn't know what to do."

"Yeah." Brandi gave me a sympathetic look. "Plus, Hunter is here. Zen is still being a jerk about you dating his partner. You probably thought the date would help you move on."

Relief made me break out into a smile. "Thank you. Exactly. All of that. But now I feel like I've hurt Hunter."

"Maybe Hunter should put on his big boy undies and stand up to Zen," Jonah said.

"He's right." Brandi nodded. "Either Hunter confronts Zen, or he has to face the consequences of losing you to a handsome doctor."

"Or losing you to anybody, really," Jonah said. "If he can't do that, he doesn't have the right to be with you."

"And you," Brandi pointed at me, "have the right to move on and be with someone who is willing to fight for you and—"

Hunter came back in and shut the door behind him.

He stopped and stared. "Hey."

"Hey." My cheeks warmed. Had he overheard our conversation?

"I'm going to hit the hay." Hunter made his way to the room he was sleeping in. "Good night."

I swallowed. "Good night."

CHAPTER 17

After we'd purchased our funeral attire at the mall, the five of us rushed to get ready. I'd found a modest black dress with short sleeves. I fashioned my hair into a low bun and slipped my feet into a pair of red espadrilles. Even a funeral needed a pop of color.

When I got to the living room, Zen and Hunter were already there. Jonah was just coming out of his room, looking appropriately dressed in fitted black trousers, light blue shirt, and a tie.

"That's the most dressed up I've seen you since we left Opulent." I hugged him. "You look nice."

"So do you." Jonah pointed at my shoes. "Those are fab."

"Thanks."

Before I could acknowledge Hunter and Zen, Brandi appeared.

"You look beautiful," I said. "I love the white piping on that navy dress."

She smiled, but I could tell she was distracted.

"You seem nervous."

Brandi clutched my hand. "I'm not sure how to act. I didn't know Arnold that well. I want to comfort Ray, but I don't want to meet his family this way, you know? I mean, I want to meet them, but under better circumstances."

"I totally understand. It'll be okay. Just be there for Ray and you will be fine."

"Promise?" Brandi looked at me with her dark eyes.

I sighed. "No. I don't know that it will be fine. But I hope it is."

We all filed out the front door in a somber manner.

Zen opened the door of his large unmarked car. "Can you guys all fit in the back?"

"Sure." Brandi followed Jonah inside. "I'm short. I can fit in the middle."

I squeezed in next to Brandi and shut the door. "Let's do this."

✳✳✳

When we got to the small church, the parking lot was full.

Hunter pointed ahead. "There's a spot along the street. It's not too far to walk back to the church."

Zen maneuvered the sedan into the tight space between a large Suburban and an old 1970s VW bus. I was impressed with my big brother's parking skills. I wasn't sure I'd be able to park even my little Prius in the same spot.

Hunter hopped out of the front seat and opened my car door, earning a sideways glance from Zen.

"Watch your head," Hunter said, helping me out. "You don't want to give yourself another concussion."

"That isn't something I want to relive." I smiled. In the suit I'd picked for him at the mall, he looked so very handsome.

127

Zen cleared his throat. "Come on, sis." He linked my arm with his. "I want you to keep you focused on the people from your rafting trip—if any of them decide to attend, that is. I'm sticking close, so you can fill me in on who everyone is."

"Got it." I let him lead me into the little white church, with Hunter, Brandi, and Jonah following close behind.

I estimated the light, bright church held about two hundred people. Two rows of pews allowed for an aisle down the middle. A dark coffin with the lid propped open was situated near the altar.

Brandi caught sight of Ray and rushed over to him. Before she could reach him, Astrid appeared out of nowhere.

"Ray!" She swooped in ahead of Brandi and wrapped her arms around his neck. She was a good three inches taller than him, and I was struck by how powerful she looked even in a floral dress.

Brandi's face fell.

Zen leaned in close to me. "Who is that?"

"Astrid. She's an Olympic athlete. She's been on several of Ray's rafting excursions," I whispered. "She was the one I saw with a married man at the play."

"Oh, Ray, I'm so sorry about your cousin. You must be devasted." Astrid's Swedish accent was suddenly more pronounced than I remembered it from the rafting trip.

She straightened his tie and pulled an imaginary hair off his jacket lapel.

"Thank you, Astrid. I'm holding up." Ray gently pushed her away and noticed Brandi behind Astrid's muscular shoulders.

"Brandi!" He went to her and hugged her tightly. "I'm so glad you could come."

Brandi went from looking forlorn to radiant. Then she must've realized she was there for a funeral. Her expression turned somber. "I'm sorry about Arnold. This must be quite a shock to all of you."

Astrid narrowed her eyes at Brandi. "What are you doing here?" She turned her gaze to Jonah and me. "And them? You barely know Ray and Arnold."

I cleared my throat. "Hello, Astrid. Nice to see you too."

Jonah blurted out, "Ray has an office next to ours in Seattle. He and Brandi are dating."

Astrid stared down at Brandi. "Ray is dating her?"

Just then, Carlson and his wife, Marlena, walked toward us.

Marlena glared at Astrid. Astrid glared at Carlson.

"This is dramatic," Hunter whispered behind me. "Where's the popcorn?"

I looked down at my toes so no one would notice my smile.

Ray put his arm around Brandi's waist. "Come on. I want to introduce you to my family."

The pair left the rest of us standing and gawking at one another. I decided to break the ice. "Astrid, Carlson, Marlena, this is my friend, Jonah, and my brother Zen—and his partner, Hunter. They're homicide detectives."

The three angry river rafters laid their eyes on the two detectives and their demeanor changed almost like magic.

"Uh, nice to meet you." Carlson shook Hunter and Zen's hands. I noticed he squeezed their hands tightly because Zen actually winced while the man had him in his grip.

Astrid turned on the charm. "Hello, detectives. Pleased to make your acquaintance."

Again, her Swedish accent seemed more pronounced around men. Did she do that on purpose or was it just her subconscious way to manipulate the opposite sex?

Regardless, I was quite sure that Hunter and Zen were on to her. At least I hoped they were. Because Astrid was a stunning specimen.

I eyed Hunter. What did he think of her?

Hunter's face betrayed nothing. His detective mode had been switched on, and he seemed both passive and alert.

The sound of someone clearing his throat startled me. I turned to see who it was. "Joe!" I gave the tall, older man a hug.

He had sat next me at our dinner at the hotel the night before we embarked on our rafting trip. Even though he'd talked my ear off at the dinner, I liked his affable manner and adventurous spirit.

"Glad I could be here." He said hello to the other rafters and introduced himself to my brother and Hunter.

When I realized that the service was about to start, I tugged on Jonah's sleeve. "Let's go sit down."

We chose a pew in the back. From our vantage point, we could observe the people who'd been on the rafting trip and keep a watch out for anything out of the ordinary.

The doors of the church behind us were propped open, allowing the warm breeze to caress our shoulders. It somehow made the funeral less gloomy.

A low buzzing sound made me look over my shoulder. A green June bug the size of a drone rumbled down the aisle and flew off toward one of the large stained-glass windows on the side. I shuddered. Giant insects were not my thing.

The minister stood by the altar. He opened his arms in a gesture for everyone to be seated and the service began.

From my seat, I could see Ray sitting in the front pew with Brandi and the rest of his family. A woman who I thought might be Arnold's mother sobbed and dabbed at her face with a white lace handkerchief.

We stood to sing a hymn. Zen and I didn't know any hymns—it wasn't like our parents ever brought us to a church service of any kind. They believed that God was everywhere and in all living things. Dad always said that nature was his church, and that was one thing we could agree on.

"You may be seated," the minister said.

Ray stood up and went to the podium. "As cousins whose parents were very close, Arnold and I grew up together. When I tried out for premier soccer, Arnold did too. We played for two years, until I got bored and decided to join the swim team instead. Guess what Arnold did?"

The parishioners laughed, breaking the tension in the sorrow-filled church.

Ray laughed too. "You guessed it. Arnold dropped soccer and took up swimming. At times, he was like a pesky—but endearing—little brother. He always wanted to tag along with me and my friends everywhere we went."

Interesting. I felt that Arnold had been a bit that way during the rafting trip, except for the few times I'd seen him argue with Ray. Then he'd seemed frustrated and almost whiny. I guess that was similar to the relationship between cousins who were as close as siblings; the younger one was always trying to measure up to the older one.

"So, when I started my river rafting business, Arnold was quick to jump onboard—pardon the pun."

Another round of quiet laughter rippled through the room.

"He was always ready to guide a rafting trip in a new location," he continued. "Always up for making new partnerships with other outdoor recreation companies to see how we could provide an even better service for our customers. He was quickly learning the ropes and wanted to contribute wherever he could, including the desire to expand our business nationally."

Arnold's mom let out one loud sob.

Ray glanced at his aunt and gave her a reassuring nod.

"I'm a little more risk-adverse and careful than Arnold is—was." Ray paused a moment and took a deep breath. "I tend to play it safer than he did—at least when it came to financial matters. But I admired his drive and his wish to grow the business."

He addressed Arnold's parents. "Arnold was a good man. I will miss him. I hope I can carry the spirit of his ambitions into everything I do going forward."

Ray stepped away from the microphone and leaned over to hug some of his family members. Once he was seated, the minister led us in a prayer.

A large woman wearing a floral dress took her place at the front and positioned the microphone at the right height. The organist began to play, and the woman at the microphone sang a moving but pitchy version of Ave Maria.

While she sang, I noticed that Zen and Hunter's eyes were constantly scanning the congregation. I needed to follow their lead and do the same—especially if I wanted to learn how to be a private detective.

Sitting about halfway down the length of the church in a pew on the right side, I focused on Joe, Astrid, Carlson, and Marlena. They were all sitting relatively close together on the bench, but Marlena sat in a rigid manner, stonily focused on the casket. Interesting. I knew she was more than upset that her husband had taken an interest in Astrid. So why was she here? Especially since she probably expected Astrid to attend Arnold's funeral.

The song ended, and the singer went back to her seat in the second row.

The minister was back at the altar. "Let us pay our respects to the departed. Please line up on the right for the viewing."

Quiet murmurs broke the silence as everyone shuffled out of their seats and made their way to the casket.

I scurried ahead of my brother and friends and stood two people behind the other rafting clients. My antennae were up. Astrid had seemed so petty and weird earlier. Now that I thought about it, she'd been acting strangely since the moment I'd met her. I wanted to keep an eye on her.

Marlena was next in line to view the body. She barely looked down at the casket. Instead, she walked stiffly past, made her way down the middle aisle, and slid into her row to take a seat.

Carlson strode forward to view Arnold's prone form. He lingered for a brief moment, murmured something unintelligible and then took a seat next to his wife.

Joe hesitated for a moment before he approached the coffin. He bowed his head in silent prayer as he stood alongside the deceased. He took a deep breath and let it out—I could tell he was upset and trying to come to terms with Arnold's death.

As Astrid approached the coffin, the low humming of the June bug that had flown in earlier caught my attention. Where was it? I turned my head to look, but the buzzing stopped.

The congregation was also craning their necks, nervous that the large bug would make a reappearance. When I returned my gaze to Astrid, she was standing very close to the casket. I gasped. Was she slipping something into the breast pocket of Arnold's suit? I had to know what she'd put in there—maybe it was some sort of clue.

When Astrid went back to her seat, I waited for the other two people ahead of me to pay their respects. Then I headed to the casket, wondering how I could remove whatever was in Arnold's pocket without everyone noticing.

I leaned over the casket and peered inside. Arnold looked like a wax version of himself, but with a better wardrobe. His brown hair was perfectly styled and there was no stubble on his cheeks or chin. The dark suit he wore looked new. I noticed the handkerchief in the breast pocket was not quite perfectly folded, probably because Astrid had disturbed it when she put something inside.

The buzzing from the June bug suddenly resurfaced and broke the reserved silence in the church. Several parishioners exclaimed and stood up, swiping at the humming monstrosity. Now that everyone was preoccupied, it was my chance to see what Astrid had placed in Arnold's pocket.

I reached inside and felt something flat and round. I quickly palmed it, straightened the handkerchief, and shoved the object into my bra.

Without any warning, the June bug buzzed loudly, hovering inches from my face. It flew straight at me. I reared back, shrieking and batted at it wildly.

A roar of concern rose from the congregation.

As the green demon came at me again, my reflexes took over. I lashed out with all my might, employing some of the moves I'd learned in Hunter's self-defense class. Unfortunately, the coffin, not the bug, was the unlucky recipient of my defensive moves.

It wobbled from side to side. Scrambling, I reached to steady it, but to no avail. It tipped over with a loud crash—directly on top of me.

I found myself flat on my back, legs splayed out in front of me. Arnold's body draped over my midsection, his cold white hand laying right across my breast. The congregation had gone still.

The smell of formaldehyde and disinfectant flooded my nostrils. Oh god, oh god, oh god. There was a dead man on top of me.

A high-pitched scream of shock and grief rose above the stillness. I had no doubt that it came from Arnold's mother.

CHAPTER 18

It wasn't *my* funeral, but I pretty much wanted to die.

The congregation was awash in whispers and exclaims of horror as people scrambled to set the casket back on the stand. Hunter, Zen, and Jonah delicately lifted Arnold's body off me and indelicately plunked him back in his coffin.

I wished I could crawl into my own coffin. I needed to escape the humiliation I was experiencing now that the shock of the moment had worn off.

Hunter's face hovered over mine. "Are you hurt?"

"Only my pride," I muttered.

He held out a hand and helped me to my feet. "Are you sure you're all right?"

I smoothed down my dress and looked around at the chaos in every direction. "I'm okay." I looked around the sanctuary. The parishioners' eyes flicked back and forth between me and the fuss flurrying around Arnold's casket. My heart fluttered with anxiety. "Can we get out of here? I need some air."

"Sure. Of course." Hunter took my hand and ushered me out a side exit door.

I stood outside on a patch of grass, underneath a cherry tree. Breathing deeply, I let the warm late summer breeze wash the stench of embarrassment off me.

A stray strand of hair which had escaped my bun during the casket debacle blew across my face. Hunter reached out and tucked it behind my ear.

"So, that was awkward," he said, tipping his chin toward the church. "What exactly were you doing with your hand in Arnold's casket? I saw you reach inside before that weird bug attacked you."

I took in a deep breath and let it out slowly. "I saw Astrid put something in Arnold's breast pocket. I needed to find out what it was."

He raised his eyebrows. "What did you discover?"

"Funny you ask that. I didn't have a chance to look at it. I was too busy fighting off a giant bug and traumatizing Arnold's family." I reached into my own breast pocket, aka my bra, pulled out the disc-shaped object, and stared at it.

"A poker chip?" Hunter took it from me and studied it.

"That's weird. Why would Astrid put a poker chip in Arnold's pocket?" I asked.

Before Hunter could answer, Zen, Jonah, and Brandi came bursting through the side door.

"What the hell was that all about?" Zen raked his fingers through his short hair.

"Are you okay?" Brandi ran to me and gave me a hug.

"That was quite the performance." Jonah grinned. "I can quite confidently say that was the most memorable funeral I've ever been to. One for the books."

I scowled at him. "I didn't do it for your entertainment."

Jonah shrugged. "I know. But I thank you anyway."

I turned to Brandi. "Can you please tell Ray that I am so, so sorry I ruined Arnold's funeral? I just can't go back in there and face him and his family right now."

"Seriously, sis," Zen said. "What were you thinking?"

"She saw Astrid put this in Arnold's pocket. I'd say she did some pretty good detective work." Hunter held the poker chip in his palm for Zen to see.

Zen took it and frowned. "Interesting."

"Maybe Astrid and Arnold played cards together," Jonah said.

"Or maybe Astrid owed Arnold some gambling money," Brandi said.

"Maybe Arnold owed her money." I took the poker chip out of Zen's hand. "And this little memento was to show him that he paid for his debt with his life."

Hunter stared at me. "You might be on to something."

"Thanks." I looked back down at the chip in my hand. "I wouldn't be surprised to learn that Arnold was a gambler. Maybe he was in way over his head."

"You think someone killed him because he owed them money?" Jonah asked.

"It's possible," Zen answered.

"I wonder if Ray knows anything about this?" Brandi looked back at the church. "Not to mention Astrid. She obviously knows something."

"Let's go find out." Zen turned to open the door we'd come out of. "After you."

I hesitated. The last thing I wanted to do was go back in there and face more humiliation. But my curiosity got the better of me. I couldn't not know what this was all about. The investigative side of me drew me back inside.

***

The casket was closed.

The congregation continued singing the last notes of a hymn as we entered. I positioned myself behind my brother against the wall and hoped Arnold's family wouldn't spot me.

Ray went to the podium. "Thank you all for coming. It means a lot to our family that you cared enough for Arnold to see him off on his next adventure. God bless."

With that, everyone rose from the pews and slowly made their way out of the church. People were still whispering about the crazy lady who had wrestled with the dead guy. My cheeks burned, and I hung my head low to avoid eye contact with anyone.

"Astrid isn't here," Brandi said. "She must've slipped out after the incident."

I looked up, hoping no one would notice my red face. "What about Carlson and the others?"

"Nope." Jonah pointed at the door. "I didn't see them either. I think they must've gone with Astrid."

Once people had cleared out, only Ray remained. Arnold's family and some of the guests had left for the cemetery, where he would be buried. Four men, who were either staff from the funeral home or pallbearers, carried Arnold's casket out of the sanctuary.

I swallowed hard. It was time to apologize. But I needed my entourage for support and encouragement. "Can you guys come with me? I need to tell Ray I'm sorry."

Together, we made our way over to where Ray was talking with the minister.

When Ray saw us approach, he said something to the clergyman, who then turned to leave.

Taking a deep breath, I made eye contact with Ray. "I just wanted to say I'm so very sorry for what happened… for what I did. I wish I could take it all back, but I can't." I bit my lip. "I'm really, really, really sorry."

Ray nodded. "It's all right, Clarity. What happened was an accident. It could've happened to anyone. That bug was—huge."

Relief rushed through me. "Yeah, it was the scariest bug I've ever seen. And loud? Boy, was it loud. I mean—"

"Shhh," Jonah said behind me. "Stop. Ray gets it."

I let out a breath. "All right."

Hunter cleared his throat. "One thing that we haven't mentioned is that Clarity witnessed Astrid putting something in Arnold's pocket. Would you happen to know why she would've put this in your cousin's casket?" He held out the poker chip for Ray to see.

Ray frowned. "A poker chip?"

"Was Arnold a gambler?" Zen asked.

"I don't think so," Ray answered, "but it's a possibility. Arnold was terrible with money. It's one of the reasons I'd resisted letting him become a partner in my business."

"Terrible with money in what way?" I asked.

"He was always needing money to help promote our rafting business and what-not. When he first asked, I gave him ten thousand dollars to use for promotions and marketing. But I never saw the results. When I asked to see receipts for where the money was spent, he couldn't produce them. He always had an excuse. Like, his car needed new brakes or his computer died. It was always something."

"What did you do?" Brandi asked.

"I stopped giving him money. I took the responsibility of marketing into my own hands, and as a result, my business grew."

"You said he wanted to become a partner?" I asked. "Like buy into the business?"

Ray nodded. "He wanted a fifty-fifty partnership."

"And you didn't like that?" Hunter asked.

"No. Like I said, I didn't trust Arnold with finances. There was no way I was going to let him tank my business. I've worked too hard for that."

I remembered something Joe had told me during our dinner at The Black Swan. "Didn't he try to start his own rafting business?"

"Yeah, that's true." Ray looked uncomfortable. "But it was a disaster. He tried luring some of my employees away, and he did manage to hire a few. When they didn't get their paychecks, they came back to me with their tails tucked between their legs."

"Interesting." Zen scribbled something into his notebook.

The doors at the front of the church darkened.

I turned to see what was blocking the light. Two uniformed officers stood in the threshold. They walked toward us.

"Ray Nielsen?" one of the officers said.

"Yes?" Ray answered.

"You're under arrest for the murder of Arnold Thatcher."

CHAPTER 19

"You're arresting Ray?" Brandi stepped forward, her brows furrowed. "That's ridiculous! Ray wouldn't kill his cousin!"

Zen put a hand on her shoulder. "Easy, Brandi. Let them do their jobs."

"But he's not guilty!" Brandi started forward, but Zen pulled her back.

Hunter turned to her. "Zen and I will go with them and see what we can do. Don't worry."

We watched them leave the church with Ray in handcuffs.

Brandi let out a defeated groan. "I can't believe this."

I put my arm around her and led her to a pew. "Here. You should sit for a moment and take deep breaths."

Brandi begrudgingly sat.

Several emotions crossed her face within a matter of seconds. First shock, then grief, and then anger. Uh oh. An angry Brandi was not easy to talk down off a ledge.

"How dare they arrest Ray in a church? What if his family had been here?" She waved her arms and paced as she ranted.

"I know, I know," I soothed. "They'll let him go soon. I'm sure of it."

"How do you know that?" Her face had gone a shade of red I'd only seen at the Nordstrom makeup counter. Mac Russian Red was it?

"Deep breaths," I told her. "Ray isn't guilty, so of course they'll let him go."

She forced herself to breathe and closed her eyes. "You're right. They will let him go. He didn't do anything wrong."

"That's right." I looked at Jonah and jerked my head toward Brandi. "Do something," I mouthed.

"Let's go back to the farm and play with the puppies," Jonah said. "You need some fur therapy."

"Fur therapy," Brandi repeated, opening her eyes. "Yes. That sounds nice."

We left the church and walked to where we'd parked. Zen and Hunter's sedan wasn't there.

"Crap," I said. "I forgot that we carpooled. How are we going to get back to my mom and dad's?"

Jonah took out his phone and a second later he said, "We've got an Uber coming. He's just right around the corner."

"That's what I love about you." I grinned at him, momentarily forgetting all the stuff that had gone down during the funeral. "You're resourceful."

"And speedy," Brandi offered.

Only two minutes went by before a black sedan arrived at the curb. Jonah checked to make sure that the make of the car and the description of the driver matched what the app had promised. We climbed inside and were soon dropped off at my parents' place.

Relief washed over me the minute I set foot on the lush grass in front of the house. That was weird. I almost felt like it was home—even though I much preferred city life.

But when the herd of goats came rushing to greet us, the warm feeling left me, and I almost jumped back into the Uber. Unfortunately, it was already backing out of the driveway and heading to wherever the next customer was.

Terrified that the goats were out to give me another concussion, I raced into the B&B and down the hall to my room. I wanted to collapse on the bed and take a nap, but I knew Brandi needed me.

I changed into a pair of shorts and a T-shirt and went back to hang out with Brandi and Jonah.

When I got to the living room, no one was there. I wandered outside and heard voices coming from the patio area. Brandi, Jonah, Mom, and Dad were sitting outside. The two puppies were in Brandi's lap, and for the first time all day, Brandi looked somewhat happy. Jolie, the all-supreme and all-knowing animal whisperer, was standing in front of Jonah, her chin on his knee.

"She likes me." He grinned.

I laughed. "I'm pretty sure she likes everybody."

Mom's smile lit up her face. "Right on. Jolie loves everyone, and I think it's contagious. I dig having you all here. This is the best couple of days I've had in a long, long time."

"Aw, that's sweet, Mom." I sat next to her. "Thanks for hosting us."

Her eyes got a little misty, and she pretended to swat away a fly. "How would you like some lavender iced tea and some chocolate zucchini cake?"

"Sounds yummy." And I had to admit, it did sound yummy. It reminded me of my childhood. Mom always made that cake for birthdays and family celebrations. Plus, I was super glad there wasn't any wheatgrass in it.

"Great. I'll bring it right out." She got up and went into the kitchen.

Brandi shook her head. "Clarity, you are so lucky to come from such a warm and loving family. I wish I'd grown up more like this."

I raised my eyebrows. "Really?" It suddenly occurred to me that I didn't know much about her childhood years.

"Yeah." She sighed and ran her fingers through the puppies' fur. "My mom and dad got divorced when I was two years old. My brother and I had to go back and forth—one week at Dad's house and one week in Mom's tiny apartment. We had to schlep our stuff between the two households. Neither place felt like home."

"I'm sorry, Brandi. That sounds awful," I said.

Jonah nodded. "I'm sorry, too. How come you never told us?"

She shrugged. "I don't know. It just makes me sad to talk about it."

Jolie moved her chin from Jonah's lap to Brandi's knee.

"Looks like you've got yourself an emotional support animal," Dad said.

Brandi laughed and scratched the little goat between the ears. "She does seem to sense people's emotions, doesn't she?"

"And animals," Dad offered. "She's got a gift."

Mom appeared in the doorway. "Darren, can you help me carry the food and drinks out?"

"Sure, Babe."

"I'll help, too." I got up and followed my parents inside.

Mom had sliced the cake into nice thick pieces. I stuck my finger in the frosting, just like I did when I was little.

"Clarity, that's not cool," she scolded. But the twinkle in her eye told me she wasn't mad.

Dad and I carried plates of cake out to my friends. Mom grabbed the pitcher of lavender iced tea and went back in for cups.

Once we were settled, we dug in. It was so delicious, I almost died.

A car rambled down the road toward us. It was a silver Porsche. My stomach sank.

Mom's face lit up. "Dr. Strong is here! Isn't that nice, Clarity!"

I eyed her suspiciously. "Mom, did you arrange this?"

She blinked. "Who, me?"

I bit back a growl. "Mom…"

The car came to a stop, a haze of dust floating through the late afternoon air. Nathan got out, looking handsome in dark gray slacks and a button-down shirt and tie. His million-watt smile lit up his face when he caught sight of me.

"Clarity! You're not wearing that out on our date, are you?"

I looked down at my T-shirt and shorts. "Date?"

"Yeah. Your mom said you were up for a night at the casino!"

I glared at Mom. "Oh, she did, did she?"

Mom's eyes twinkled again. "I just figured you'd want to go. Why don't you change into something more suitable, honey?"

My eyes met Brandi's and then Jonah's. They seemed as shocked as I was that Mom had pulled something so sneaky.

Nathan watched me expectantly. "We'll need to leave in a few minutes if we want to beat traffic."

I was about to protest when my thoughts flitted to the poker chip I'd extracted from Arnold's pocket. If Arnold had gambled somewhere nearby, perhaps I could find out some information from the employees of the casino...

"I'll go get ready right now."

Out of the corner of my eye, I noticed Jonah and Brandi's mouths hanging open. I winked at them and darted into the B&B to get dressed for the evening.

CHAPTER 20

Was it tacky to wear the dress I wore to a funeral out on a date?

It was the only dress I had with me, so it would have to do. I put on some red lipstick, brushed out my long dark hair, and spritzed some perfume on my neck and wrists. There.

Before I went down the hall to meet up with Nathan, I texted Brandi and Jonah. "Get dressed and meet me there."

Brandi texted back. "Which casino?"

"Don't know," I responded. "I'll text you when I find out. Let's do some snooping into Arnold's extra-curricular activities."

Brandi sent me the thumbs up emoji.

When I met Nathan downstairs, Brandi and Jonah had already gone to their rooms to get ready. Mom and Dad were talking Nathan's ear off about marijuana farming.

"It's just a shame that everyone can sell the damn stuff now. Our crop was near perfect until the neighbors started growing their crop. Their stuff is sub-par, if you know what I mean." Mom shook her head. "And then it started hybridizing with our crop. It's not the quality it used to be."

Nathan's frozen grin told me he was humoring them. "I bet that's frustrating for you."

"Damn right," Dad said. "We had to move all the plants into a couple of greenhouses. The good thing is that the goats can't get into it. No more overdoses in the herd to worry about."

"Every cloud has a silver lining." Mom held out the pitcher of iced tea. "Care for some before you head out?"

Nathan shook his head. "No thank you."

His head turned toward me as I approached. "Wow. You look—wow."

"You look nice, honey." Mom got up and kissed my cheek. "Have fun and don't do anything I wouldn't do."

"Which means I can do just about anything," I muttered under my breath.

"What was that?" Dad asked.

"Nothing. I'll see you guys later. Don't wait up." I winked at Mom. Even though I was mad at her for setting me up once again, I was itching to find out more about Arnold's secret habit.

Once we were settled in the car and on the main road, I asked, "So, which casino are we going to?"

"The Skagit River Casino." He glanced over at me with a smile.

"I've never heard of that one." I put my hand inside my purse, wondering how I would text Brandi and Jonah without him seeing what I was doing.

"It just opened a couple of months ago. I normally go to the Lucky Clover Casino. I've only been to this one once before. It's nice. You'll love it."

The sun was still bright, and I wondered how many people would be gambling in the late afternoon. I wasn't a gambler, but

I'd always imagined that people who gambled did so in the late hours of the night with a drink in hand.

The Porsche accelerated down a windy road, and Nathan gunned it when the street straightened out. I felt a pang of fear as we flew down the mostly untraveled stretch of highway.

Nathan laughed. "Hope I'm not scaring you. I like my cars fast." He gave me a long look.

Was he going to say, "I like my women fast, too"? God, I hoped he wasn't thinking what I thought he was thinking. A prickle of unease made my heart beat faster.

My phone buzzed. It was a text from Brandi. "WHICH CASINO?"

"Who's texting you?" He asked as I took my phone out of my purse.

"My friend, Brandi."

"Oh."

I texted back, "A new one called Skagit River Casino."

"Thanks," she responded. "We're on our way."

I felt a little better knowing that my friends would be there watching my back. I was starting to get another weird vibe from Nathan.

✳✳✳

It took a good thirty minutes to drive to the casino. We'd hit rush hour and there was an accident on the freeway.

Conversation between Nathan and me was one-sided.

"When I finished my undergrad degree at Stanford, I went into medical school at Johns Hopkins. It wasn't exactly a party school, so I had to sow my oats in a different kind of way, if you know what I mean."

I stared at him. "No, I don't know what you mean."

He glanced at me, his eyes twinkling. "Maybe I shouldn't tell you."

"Maybe I don't want to know." I looked out the window. He was getting creepier.

Nathan chuckled. "Let's save it for another time, then."

As if, I thought. There wasn't going to be another time as far as I was concerned.

The casino sign was lit up and mounted on a landscaped little hill. River rocks formed the base of the sign, giving it a folksy but expensive look. It reminded me of Disney's California Adventure park.

Nathan took my hand in his, and my first instinct was to pull it away. But I had a job to do, so for now, I needed to play along.

When we walked into the entrance and lobby, I looked all around, admiring the décor.

The pillars in the lobby were all made of solid wood which was echoed in the wooden beams in the soaring ceiling overhead. Though the casino was by all means smaller than the popular casinos in Vegas, it seemed grand.

We passed the hotel check-in desk and walked by a river rock wall fountain, which tinkled serenely in the twinkling light of the lanterns affixed to the rustic walls.

From there, we entered the casino itself, with hundreds of machines chiming and blinking bright lights. The atmosphere was so drastically different from the entrance, it felt jarring. Instead of feeling calm and peaceful, I felt wide awake and alert.

Nathan tugged on my hand. "Want to grab a bite of dinner before we play?"

My stomach rumbled in response. "Sure."

He pulled me along the path on the outskirts of the machines to a large restaurant which seemed to have the same lodge-like feel as the lobby. Immediately, I felt more relaxed.

"Is this okay? Or we could go to the bar instead." Nathan put his hand on the small of my back. "Whatever you'd like."

"No, this is great."

A hostess materialized immediately. "Just the two of you tonight?"

Nathan grinned. "That's right. Just the two of us."

Ugh. This was getting a little too cozy for me. But I still needed to find out if Arnold had been a regular here.

The hostess led us to a table next to a window where we could look into the casino. "I'll send your server right over to take your order. Can I get you some drinks while you wait?"

Nathan nodded. "I'd like a whiskey sour. Clarity?"

I wanted to stay alert and not let alcohol cloud my judgment or ability to work, but I thought it would look weird if I didn't order a drink. "A glass of Cabernet would be great." I would just sip slowly and stop if I felt the effects of the wine.

The hostess disappeared, and Nathan reached for my hand. "I'm so happy to spend this night with you. I'm a lucky guy."

Spend the night with him? Did he mean...?

A waitress appeared with our drinks. She was a young blond woman with perky, and perhaps surgically, enhanced breasts. "Nathan! I haven't seen you for a week! What have you been up to? I hope you're keeping out of trouble."

Nathan smiled and looked at me. "You know me, Tiffany. I'm always on my best behavior."

Was he avoiding eye contact with her?

"That's not what you said last week. In fact, you said you were being a very, very bad boy." She giggled.

Either she was intentionally trying upset me or she was really dumb. Little did she know, I had zero interest in this schmuck.

He cleared his throat. "Tiffany, be a doll, and bring us each the shrimp salad and the clam chowder, will you?"

I frowned. I was tempted to lie and say I was allergic to seafood. He hadn't even asked me what I'd like to eat. But... I was here for a reason. I needed information.

"Anything else?" The disappointment on her face was obvious.

"No, I think that'll do, thank you." He waved her away.

Wow. He was a bigger douche than I thought.

Her eyes teared up momentarily before she turned to deliver the order to the kitchen.

I took a big gulp of my wine. "Excuse me, Nathan. I'm going to visit the ladies' room. Be back in a second."

Before he could answer, I whisked off in the direction of the restrooms. As I walked down the narrow hallway, I glanced into the kitchen, where Tiffany had gone to take the order to the chef. Her big blue eyes were filled with tears, and I could tell she was trying hard to maintain her composure. I motioned for her to follow me.

Inside the restroom, I waited for her to enter. When she did, I put my hand on her arm. "I'm so sorry Nathan treated you the way he did. Guys like that are jerks. You deserve better than that."

She sniffed. "How did you know—"

"It was obvious." I cut her off before she could say anything further. "Choose a guy who treats you well. Don't settle for anything less."

She nodded and wiped a tear from her cheek. "But why are you with him, then?"

I shook my head. "He thinks I'm into him, but I'm not. My mom set us up. She didn't know that he's not a nice guy. But listen, can you tell me if you've seen this guy here before?" I showed her a picture on my phone. It was a photo of Ray and Arnold that I'd taken on our rafting trip. They were standing together, deep in conversation about something.

"I don't recognize this one." She pointed at Ray. "But this guy I recognize. His name is Arnold. He comes here a lot and sometimes plays in the big stakes games—poker mostly."

Suspicions confirmed. "Where are the high stakes games played? In the main casino?"

"No, those are played behind the main casino. There's a VIP section in the back. You enter on the right side, behind the roulette wheels."

I smiled. "Thank you, Tiffany. You've been very helpful."

"What is this all about? Is Arnold in trouble?" she asked.

"No. Unfortunately, Arnold was killed over the weekend. I'm just trying to learn more about his background and what might have led to his death."

Her eyes grew wide. "Arnold was murdered?"

I nodded. "It's tragic. But I would appreciate it if you could keep this quiet for a few days while we sort through the details."

"Oh, absolutely. Arnold was a real nice guy. I hope they catch the person who did that to him. Do you think someone here did it?" She bit her lip.

"I don't know. I'm just trying to learn everything I can."

"Are you a detective?" she asked.

I hesitated. "Private investigator." That was the first time I'd ever used those words to describe my occupation. It didn't feel real. Was I really a P.I.? I hadn't received my certification yet, but I would shortly.

Tiffany checked the time on her phone. "I better get back to work. Thanks for your kind words. I hope Nathan doesn't trick you into sleeping with him. He's pretty charming, but I don't think he's a very nice person."

"You've got good instincts. Take care of yourself, Tiffany."

She opened the door and let it swing shut.

I looked in the mirror and reapplied my red lipstick. So, Arnold had been a regular here. A regular who often played poker with the high rollers. Was his gambling linked to his murder? I needed to know more.

When I returned to the table, Nathan looked at his expensive wristwatch. "Are you feeling all right? You've been gone over ten minutes."

Slightly irked that he'd been timing me, I answered, "Oh, I'm fine. I just had to freshen up so I could look my best for you."

His wolfish grin shone in the dim light. The candle on the table cast shadows on under his cheekbones and highlighted his bright blue eyes. "Well, then. It was worth the wait."

Tiffany and another server appeared with the food and set it down in front of us. "Enjoy your meal." She looked over her shoulder and winked in my direction.

I took a bite of the chowder. Despite being irritated that he'd ordered for me, I couldn't argue with his choice in food. It was delicious.

"You like?" He put his hand on mine.

Thankfully, he'd put his hand on my left hand, not my right. I was too busy eating to swat him away. "It's very good. I didn't realize how hungry I am."

"Eat up. You'll need your strength for later."

I glanced up at him. Was he for real? The creepy vibes made my skin crawl. "For when we play the slot machines?"

He laughed. "You're funny, Clarity."

I dug into my salad and drank a small sip of wine. It tasted weird. Had Nathan put something in my drink when I'd gone to the bathroom?

I flagged down a server walking by. "Excuse me. This wine tastes off to me. Can I get a replacement? The house red is fine."

"Oh, of course. I'll bring you another." He took the glass from me and walked it back to the bar area.

I cocked an eyebrow at Nathan. "That was weird. It tasted fine before I left for the restroom."

He shrugged. Was that a hint of color in his cheeks?

The waiter returned with a fresh glass. "Sorry about that, miss."

"Thank you." I took a sip. "This is much better."

I set the glass close to me. I wasn't going to take my eyes off it, even for a minute.

CHAPTER 21

Once we finished our meal, Nathan put a plastic card on the table in front of me.

"What's this?" I turned the card over. It was a hotel room key.

"I just thought that if you'd like to get to know me better, you should have a key to my room. I got the fancy suite with the hot tub and a view of the valley."

Was this his version of the Bachelor's "fantasy suite"? The gross factor on this guy just ticked up another twenty notches.

Instead of punching him, I smiled. "No thank you. I don't think that's a good idea, considering I recently incurred a concussion. I shouldn't have had a glass of wine, come to think of it."

"Oh, right. I forgot." He shook his head and chuckled. "How's your head, by the way?"

"It's fine. But I don't want to stay out too late. I want to make sure I get enough rest."

"Let me know if you change your mind. You'd be safe with me. I am a doctor, after all."

I wanted to say that he was not a very good one, but I kept my mouth shut.

He paid the bill, and we headed out onto the floor of the casino.

A woman carrying a tray of mixed drinks sashayed by. She was tall, with light brown hair and hazel eyes. "Hello, handsome! So glad to see you." She kissed him and laid her hand on his cheek.

Nathan smiled. "Hello, Desiree."

"Wow, you seem to know everyone here." I pressed my lips together. Did he have a fling with her, too?

Nathan gently removed her hand from his cheek.

She eyed me, not in a jealous way, but in an appraising way. "This your new lady friend? She's pretty."

"Desiree, this is my date, Clarity."

"Nice to meet you. Would you like a drink?" She held the tray toward me.

"No thank you." I didn't want to get drunk and let the hoochie doctor have his way with me.

"I'll take one." He reached for a drink. "Thanks, Desiree. Catch you later." He led me to a bank of slot machines. "Want to warm up on these before we hit the poker table?"

I shrugged. "Sure. Why not?"

I noticed the people sitting at the slot machines. A purple-haired old lady was commandeering two machines simultaneously. She sat in a zombie-like trance, pulling levers and watching the cherries, lemons, and other fruits spin and spin.

"Let's try those over there." Nathan pointed to two unoccupied machines in another row.

We sat in front of the overly colorful machines, mesmerizing their prey with sounds and lights. I chose the Lord of the Rings machine, while Nathan picked one displaying James Bond brandishing a gun.

These machines were more high-tech. No levers—just buttons. I pushed the start button. I watched the images spin and stop, spin and stop, spin and stop. How was this fun?

But then three of the same images lined up, two with a 3x sticker on the top.

"A win that would satisfy a king," the feminine voice said. Was that the elf queen? Cool!

"Nice job." Nathan looked at my score. "You won two hundred dollars."

"What?" Excitement bubbled up inside me. Two hundred dollars would buy a lot of groceries. "Let's play again!"

He chuckled. "Maybe later. How about we go play a grown-up game?" He grabbed my hand and pulled me to the back of the casino, where an unassuming door was labeled VIP.

The guard standing next to the door nodded, and Nathan flashed a VIP pass. The man opened the door. "Enjoy your game. There's one starting in two minutes. One seat available."

"Thank you." Nathan put his hand at the small of my back and we stepped into a beautiful room with a large river rock fireplace dominating the back wall. There were four tables set up in the room, each with nine chairs.

Nathan sat down in the empty chair of the only table with an opening. "Hang out behind me and watch. I'm a pro."

Having never played a game of poker or any other card game besides Go Fish, I studied the people at the table. Three of them were wearing dark glasses. Was that to keep others from reading their facial expressions?

The game began.

I had a hard time following the banter between the players. Some of them joked a lot—probably to divert attention to their bluffs. Others were more serious.

My phone buzzed.

I stepped back a moment and glanced at the screen. It was Brandi. "Where are you??"

"In the VIP section. You need a badge of some sort to get in here," I texted back.

"Shoot. We're next to the roulette wheels. Can you get out of there?"

I looked around. If I left, would they let me back in here? I needed to find a way to ask questions without making a fuss at the door.

My phone vibrated again. It was my brother. "Sis, where the hell are you? Mom said you left with Nathan Strong. That guy is bad news. Tell me where you are and we'll come pick you up."

I checked to make sure that Nathan was still immersed in the game before I texted back. "At the new Skagit River Casino on Willow Road. In the VIP section. Can't get out right now. Getting info on Arnold."

A few seconds went by before he answered. "Why didn't you tell us this?"

"Because Mom set me up and there was no time to tell you." Well, that was partially true. I did have time to text Brandi. Maybe I should've texted Zen and Hunter too.

"I did a background check on that Dr. Strong. He's bad news, Clarity."

Shoot. I mean, I already sort of knew that. But was he in trouble with the police?

"What has he done?" I texted.

"Lots of stuff. Complaints from female patients. He inflated the cost of care to bilk the insurance companies, but claimed it was an honest mistake. Got off on that charge. He made a deal with his former hospital of employment to leave rather than get fired."

"You found all that out in a background check?" I didn't think that was possible.

"Nope. I have connections. Don't ask."

I sent a thumbs-up emoji. Since when did my big brother bend the rules? Perhaps I didn't know him as well as I thought I did.

Nathan shoved a stack of poker chips into the center of the table.

"Think you got a good hand there, Doc?" A guy sporting a cowboy hat grinned.

"Guess you'll just have to wait and see." He threw in an extra chip for effect.

"Looks like he has a gambling problem in addition to his other faults," I texted.

"We're heading over to the casino. Text you when we get there."

"No need. Brandi and Jonah will drive me back to Mom and Dad's."

"Okay, but call if you need us."

"Will do," I responded.

There was a roar of disgust at the table next to us. One guy was grinning ear to ear, while the other men leaned back in their chairs looking disappointed. Several of them got up and stretched. This was my chance to get some information on Arnold. I opened my photos app and located the photo of Ray's cousin I'd shown Tiffany earlier.

"Excuse me, Nathan. I'll be right back."

He barely acknowledged me as he heckled the guy across the table from him.

I slipped away and approached a short man wearing a black suit. His shirt was unbuttoned two slots too many.

"Hey, beautiful," the man drawled. "What's a pretty thing like you doing in a place like this?"

Oh my God. How original. "I'm here with him." I pointed to Nathan, who was raking in a pile of chips. He must've won that hand—or whatever that was called.

"Doc? He's no good, sweetheart. You need a quality guy like me." His eyes roved from my head to my toes—quite a feat since eye-level for him was my collar bone.

I ignored his comment and grossness and showed him the photo of Arnold. "Do you recognize this guy?"

"What, are you a cop?" He stepped back.

"No. I'm curious about this guy. I met him on a rafting trip, and he said he came here a lot."

He barked out a laugh. "That guy? That's Arnold. He's a loser. You don't want to mess around with him."

I was beginning to think he would say that about any guy who wasn't him. "What makes you say that?"

He snorted. "About a week ago, he came in here and lost about half a million bucks. In one night! I thought he was gonna have a coronary. He turned beet red and stormed out of here."

"Half a million? Where did he get all that money?" I wondered out loud.

The guy shrugged. "No idea. But I haven't seen him in here since. Maybe he learned his lesson."

"Thanks for the info. Good luck with your next game." I turned to leave.

"Hey!" he called after me. "Want to go out sometime?"

"No. As I said, I'm with him." I pointed to Nathan, who was deep in concentration over the cards in his hand.

"Eh, you have bad taste in men," he growled. "By the way, that loser, Arnold—he was a friend of that moron you're with."

I tried to keep the surprise out of my reaction. "He was?"

"Yeah. Those two have been in here every weekend since the place opened."

Interesting. Nathan had told me he'd only been here once before. I went to stand behind the good doctor once again. I wanted to ask him what his relationship to Arnold was. Nathan hadn't been at the funeral...

"Can I ask you something?" I laid a hand on his shoulder.

"Not right now. I need a drink," he said, barely glancing at me. "Can you go get me one? The server hasn't been by here in ages."

"Do you want a whiskey sour or something else?" I asked.

"That's fine. It will help me think."

Where did he get his medical degree? I'd never heard a doctor say that alcohol would help you think. And what was with his Dr. Jekyll and Mr. Hyde routine? He went from falling over himself to be cozy with me to acting like I was his personal servant.

My phone buzzed. It was Brandi again. "Jonah and I are coming in. We convinced the guard that we know you and need to talk to you."

Relief washed over me. I needed to figure out how to get out of here without Nathan pressuring to spend the night. "Yes!" I texted to her. "Get in here."

The door opened and Brandi and Jonah entered, looking out of place.

I rushed over to them and spoke quietly. "I found out that Arnold lost half a million dollars here last week."

Jonah let out a low whistle. "That's a lot of money to gamble away. Where did he get it? I thought he was trying to buy into Ray's business."

I nodded. "Me too. If he had that kind of cash, he could've just bought his partnership outright. Why would he risk it all?"

Brandi frowned. "Beats me. Ray told him he would consider letting him become a partner if he could raise $500,000. But Ray thought Arnold couldn't come up with that kind of money, so he never worried about it. But if Arnold had it…"

"Then why didn't he go straight to Ray and buy in?" My mind wandered, trying to think of an explanation.

"Clarity," Nathan said with annoyance. "You said you'd get me a drink."

Gambling sure eroded his fake charm. "Sorry. I'll be right back."

Brandi and Jonah glared at Nathan.

I flagged down a server and gave her the jerk's order.

While we waited for her to return with the drink, I glanced around the room. "There's another table finishing their game over there. Want to see if you can find out any more dirt on Arnold? I'll text you his photo."

"Sure." Brandi waited until my text came through, and then she and Jonah took off.

The server returned with the whiskey sour, and I placed it in front of Nathan. "Here you go."

"Thanks." He glugged down half of it and pushed a pile of poker chips into the center of the table.

The guy across from him grunted. "Fold." He tossed his cards on the table.

Everyone else had already folded.

Nathan grinned and slugged back the rest of his drink. "Thank you, gentlemen." He leaned forward momentarily to rake up his winnings with his arms.

"Wow. You won!" I hoped this was the end of the game. I wanted to tell him that I wasn't staying the night and didn't have any interest in seeing him again.

But apparently, the game wasn't over. Fresh cards were dealt. Crap.

"Nathan, I—"

"Shh, Clarity. Can't you see I'm concentrating?"

Brandi and Jonah motioned for me to join them.

"All we found out was that Arnold was a high-stakes wannabe. He normally played for lower stakes, like a few thousand here and there. When he lost that half a mil, that was only his second time playing with the big boys." Jonah tipped his head toward a table that had started up a new game. "They all thought Arnold was in way over his head."

"What was he thinking?" Brandi made a tsking noise. "I don't get it."

"Clarity!" Nathan barked. "I need another drink."

I clenched my jaw. "Don't worry. I'll get you one."

The server was at the far end of the room. I nearly jogged over to place Nathan's order.

When I returned, Brandi and Jonah were staring at me.

"Why are you waiting on that jerk?" Jonah squinted at the back of Nathan's head. "He doesn't deserve it."

"I know." I gave him a smug smile.

"Then why do it?" Brandi asked.

The server came by with Nathan's drink. I smiled and thanked her.

"Nathan." I stood behind him, drink in hand.

"What?" he snapped as he pushed the entirety of his winnings into the center of the table.

I looked down at his cards and winced. "Nice bluff."

The player across from him grinned and revealed his cards.

Nathan's face turned an interesting shade of red. Now he looked more sunburned than tan. He glared at me in anger. "Look what you did!"

"Oh, and Nathan," I said with a saccharine smile. "Here's your drink." I poured it ceremoniously over his head.

The men at the table erupted in laughter.

Nathan jumped up, sputtering and cursing, but I didn't stick around to see what would happen next. I grabbed Brandi's and Jonah's hands and ran for the door.

CHAPTER 22

"Geesh, what happened to the charming tanned god we met earlier?" Jonah said once we reached the parking lot. "I can't believe what a creep that guy turned into."

"Addiction will do that to a person." Brandi opened the back door of Jonah's car and climbed in.

"You think Dr. Strong is addicted to gambling?" Jonah started the car.

"Maybe. Among other things." I buckled my seatbelt.

"Like what?" Brandi asked.

"Like, it seems as though every woman we encountered in the casino has had a fling with him. No surprise he treats them like dirt, too. Zen texted me that he did a background check on the good doctor and found that he has many complaints from female patients."

"What kind of complaints?" Jonah pulled onto the main road. "Did he touch them inappropriately or worse?"

"I don't think so. Zen said something about him being overly friendly with the patients and some of the women felt uncomfortable around him."

"Creeper," Brandi muttered.

"And," I continued, "he fudged his billing records to collect more money from the insurance companies—though that charge seems to have been dropped. Who knows what went on there?"

"Wow." Jonah pulled onto the highway. "He sounds like a real catch."

"He's awful. Nathan is a regular gambler, and he also knew Arnold. I wish I'd had a chance to ask him about that before I poured a drink over his head."

"You should check with your brother to see if he knows more," Brandi said.

"You're right." I pulled out my phone and sent a text to Zen asking him if his digging into Nathan's background had revealed anything about gambling. "And can you question Dr. Strong too? I want to know if he and Arnold were really friends or if they were enemies."

While Jonah drove, I scrutinized Nathan's Instagram posts. There were pictures of him leaning on the hood of his fancy car, selfies that highlighted his bright blue eyes, and others of him with his arm casually thrown around the shoulders of pretty women. There were a few of the sunsets in the valley and shots of the tulip fields, too.

The photos didn't reveal anything too personal, and they certainly didn't give any hints toward a gambling addiction or proof he had a contentious relationship with Arnold.

Brandi checked her phone. "Nothing from Ray. I wish I knew his family better. I need to know if they got him out on bail. Can you ask Zen?"

"Sure." I texted my brother and waited for a reply.

A few seconds later, a text from Zen appeared on my screen. "Ray's bail is set at one million. Too high for his family to pay."

I gasped and showed the text to Brandi.

"Oh my God! Why is it so high?"

I bit my lip. "It's a murder charge, Brandi. Maybe the judge thinks he's a flight risk."

"He could easily hop on a boat to Canada," Jonah offered.

I shot him a hostile look. Brandi was upset enough without a comment like that.

Brandi put her head in her hands. "I can't believe this is happening."

My heart hurt for my friend. Finally, she'd found someone she had a connection with—someone she thought she could love. And now this…

"Don't worry, Brandi. We'll figure this out." I glanced at Jonah. His jaw was clenched, and I knew that he was feeling as bad for Brandi as I was.

When we pulled up to Mom and Dad's house, the twinkling lights of the outdoor seating area beckoned.

"Brandi, why don't you and Jonah sit on the patio? I'll get us something to drink."

She nodded. "Thanks. That would be great."

I slipped into Mom and Dad's kitchen and opened the fridge. There was a bowl of hummus, freshly chopped vegetables, and a pitcher of iced tea. I frowned. Brandi needed something stronger.

"Whatcha lookin' for, honey?" Dad's voice came from the doorway of the kitchen.

I jumped and put my hand to my heart. "You scared me!"

Dad chuckled. "Sorry."

"Brandi's had a hard day. I was looking for beer or something like that."

Dad's eyes lit up. "I got something much better in the barn."

I cocked an eyebrow. Was he going to offer us weed?

"Follow me." He opened the kitchen door to the backyard.

The puppies, who'd been sleeping on the floor by the couch, woke up and raised their heads. When they realized that we were going out, they sprang to their feet, tails wagging.

"Want to go outside?" I reached down to pet their soft fur. Kodiak's sharp little teeth bit into my finger. "Ouch! You little shark." I picked him up and tried to give him a stern look. But those big brown eyes… and that soft cream-colored fur.

I just couldn't be mad. I set him down and let the pups follow Dad and me out the door.

The big red barn about a hundred yards behind the house had been freshly painted. "The barn looks nice, Dad. Did you paint it yourself?"

"I had help. You know those two guys who live on Rambling Road? They like to smoke a lot of pot. But they don't always have the funds to pay their tab. I get a lot of free labor out of them."

I laughed. "You're capitalizing on someone's drug addiction?"

"Weed's habit-forming, not addictive, honey. And it's a fair trade. I'd have to pay tradesmen to do it anyway. Might as well let them pay off their debt with an honest day's work. It's a win-win situation."

The puppies were toddling after us, stopping every now and then to sniff and pee.

Once we entered the barn, Dad flicked on the lights.

The goats, which were already slumbering in the straw, woke up and bleated.

"Now, now. It's all right." His soothing voice calmed the herd, separated by twos and threes in barn stalls. "Daddy's just getting some booze for Clarity and her friends."

I giggled. "You stash your booze in the barn?"

Dad grinned. "I've got to store it somewhere." He led me to a corner of the barn where there was a mini-kitchen area. There was a short countertop with a double cabinet beneath next to a large, stainless steel fridge. He opened the door, and I peeked inside.

The racks were populated with six-packs of hard cider in glass bottles.

I lifted a six-pack out and read the name and logo printed on the packaging. "Blooming Hard Cider." There was an illustration of an obviously drunk goat drinking a bottle of cider with a straw.

"This is hilarious! I love it. Where do you sell this?"

"Oh, around." Dad took out another couple of six-packs. "There are a couple local restaurants that love this stuff. And a few mom and pop grocery stores. I can't seem to make enough of it. I sell out pretty fast. Might be time to open up that unused acre and plant more apple trees."

"Yeah! You could make a fortune!"

He shrugged. "At least enough to keep the lights on."

The puppies yipped and scratched on one of the stall doors.

"What are they doing?" I craned my neck to see what they were up to.

Dad tipped his chin in the direction of the stall. "Oh, that's where Jolie sleeps. Looks like they want a sleepover."

I walked over to the stall door and opened the latch. The puppies rushed in, tails wagging. To my surprise, Jolie was snuggled in the straw with Pumpkin. My cat was a happy camper, all stretched out in the warmth of Jolie's side. The puppies wriggled over to their furry friends and curled up into balls next to Pumpkin.

"Oh, my God. That's the cutest thing I've ever seen."

"Jolie has a way of bringing peace and harmony to everyone." Dad closed the fridge door. "I'll just take these out to your friends."

"Thanks, Dad. I'll be right there."

I leaned my elbows on the top edge of the stall door, watching the animals snuggle. Their soft snoring sounds lulled me into a feeling of well-being. I stood there for a long while and was lost in the serenity of the sleeping animals until a hand on my shoulder made me squeal and jump, my heart racing wildly.

"Sorry. Didn't mean to scare you." Hunter's voice came from behind me.

Pumpkin opened one eye and then closed it.

Hunter stepped beside me, putting his elbows on the top of the stall door as well. "Oh, man. That's all kinds of cute right there."

Being so close to him unnerved me. I turned my attention toward the sleeping animals for a second and then back to his handsome face. "Yes, it is."

His eyes darted to me, but I quickly looked back to the animals.

Oh, God. What was I doing? I shouldn't flirt with him. Nothing would ever come of it. Whatever it was. Zen had made that quite clear.

Hunter scooted in closer. "It will be fun to have our puppies grow up together. We'll have to have lots of playdates."

"Yes!" I smiled. Then I frowned. "I mean, no. I mean…"

"Clarity." He touched my arm.

I cleared my throat. "Where's Zen? Didn't you come back together?"

He didn't take his hand away. "He's having a talk with your mom." He laughed. "He's telling her not to set you up on any more dates."

I giggled. "Good. Mom doesn't always have the best judge of character. One time, when I was eighteen, she set me up with a tattoo artist she met in La Conner."

Hunter cocked an eyebrow. "What's wrong with that?"

"He was ten years older than me, for one thing. And his tattoo shop was closed down by the health and safety department because of sanitary violations. If I remember correctly, he didn't sterilize his equipment properly and some of his clients developed MRSA."

Hunter shuddered. "Yikes."

"I know, right?"

"Why did your mom think he was a good match?" Hunter's amused grin brought out his dimples.

"She was impressed that he owned his own business. She didn't think to dig into his background or even consider how old he was."

Hunter shook his head. "So, a doctor and a tattoo entrepreneur. I guess I don't measure up in her eyes."

My eyes widened. "Oh, I don't think she's even considered you because you're Zen's partner."

"Have you considered me?" His eyes fixed on mine.

My heart stopped for a moment, then restarted with a lurch. "Every day, but…"

He turned to face me and brushed the hair away from my cheek. "I know. Zen's crazy rules. But I can't deny that I have feelings for you."

I bit my lip. "I've had feelings for you from the first moment I saw you."

He tilted my chin up and kissed me. His lips were soft, but firm, and I melted into his embrace.

"Clarity!" Zen's voice boomed from the open barn door. "What the hell are you two doing?"

CHAPTER 23

Hunter and I jumped apart.

I stifled a nervous giggle. It would almost be funny if we weren't at the center of Zen's ire. Instead, I looked down at my shoes.

"I said, what the hell are you two doing?" Zen shouted.

"Zen, I'm sorry." My cheeks burned.

Hunter held out his hand. "No, Clarity. Don't apologize." Anger flashed in his eyes. "Zen, we need to talk."

Zen bristled. "Whatever you have to say, you can say in front of Clarity. You're both at fault here, as far as I'm concerned."

Hunter gave me a sideways glance.

I nodded for him to go ahead.

"Clarity and I have feelings for each other. I know you have 'rules' against this, but your rules aren't the department's rules. And no matter what happens between Clarity and me, I will always have your back. You should know that by now."

"Yeah, you say that." Zen's posture remained rigid. "But what if you two break up and you hurt her? What if subconsciously, I don't have your back?"

Hunter shook his head. "That's not who you are."

Zen flexed his jaw. "Still, I don't think you're the right fit for her."

Hunter cocked an eyebrow. "I'm not the right fit? Who are you to judge if I'm the right fit? Would you rather have her dating Dr. Strong? Is he the right fit?"

All the air seemed to leave Zen's body, and he deflated like a balloon. "No." His voice was small.

"Will anybody be the right fit for me, Zen?" I fought back angry tears. "You've disapproved of every boyfriend I've had. I know you're my protective big brother, but I'm a grown woman. I should be free to choose who I want to be with. And the fact of the matter is, I'd like to see where things go with Hunter. I like him."

I was surprised that my voice sounded strong, when inside, I felt anything but strong. I'd tried hard to respect my brother's wishes about dating his partner, but my heart wanted Hunter. I hoped Zen could understand.

Zen growled and threw up his hands. "Okay. Fine. I hope you're right. We'll talk about this in the morning." He headed for the door murmuring, "I'm going to bed."

We watched him leave, banging the wooden door shut behind him.

I took in a deep breath and let it out slowly. "That was rough."

Hunter nodded. "Yeah. I hope he can come to terms with this." He bent to kiss me lightly on the lips. "I have a lot to think about. I'm going to turn in early. It's been a long day."

"Okay." I watched him slip out into the night. Instead of feeling elated that Hunter and I would finally have a shot at a relationship, I felt drained and sad.

I took one more look at the sleeping animals, thinking how uncomplicated their lives were compared to mine, and then let myself out of the barn.

**

Brandi and Jonah had already finished their first bottle of hard cider by the time I joined them on the patio.

Brandi took one look at my face and frowned. "What happened?"

"Hunter kissed me."

Brandi squealed. "Oh, my God!"

Jonah raised his brows. "Isn't that a good thing? You've had a thing for him for a while now."

"Zen walked in on us." I looked down at my hands.

"Oh." Jonah made a face. "Awkward."

Brandi leaned forward. "Did he freak out?"

I nodded. "Yup."

Jonah opened a bottle of cider and handed it to me. "Here."

I accepted the bottle gratefully and took a sip. I was surprised at how delicious it was. The crisp flavor of apples sweetened with a lingering hint of honey.

"So, then what?" Brandi reached for her second bottle and held it clutched to her chest.

"Basically, Zen told Hunter that he didn't want his partner dating his sister because if anything bad happened between us, they might not have each other's back."

"Really?" Brandi raised an eyebrow.

"And not only that, Zen said Hunter wasn't a good 'fit' for me. Hunter asked if Dr. Strong was a better fit—which shut Zen up. I told Zen that it was apparent he wouldn't approve of any man who was interested in me."

"Whoa." Jonah cringed. "You're probably right. He's very protective of you. Almost like a dad."

I sighed. "I know. It's super annoying. In the end, he said we should talk in the morning."

"What did Hunter say after that?" Brandi said.

"After Zen left the barn, Hunter kissed me again and said he was turning in."

"Well, at least he didn't give into Zen." Brandi opened her cider and took a sip. "He stood up for himself, but more importantly, he stood up for you."

"True. I just want everyone to get along, you know what I mean?" I leaned back into the cushion. My stomach churned as I thought about talking to Zen in the morning.

"Not to change the subject," Jonah said, "but did Zen or Hunter say anything about interviewing Dr. Strong? Have they done that yet?"

I shrugged. "I forgot to ask. Everything was so weird. I'm sure if they'd talked to him, they would've said something about it."

"We can ask them in the morning." Brandi checked her phone and let out a sigh. "I keep checking my phone, expecting there to be a text from Ray. Then I remember that he's in jail. They don't let you have your phone in jail, do they?"

I bit my lip. "No, they don't."

Jonah took another bottle of cider for himself. "This calls for more cider and a change of subject."

"Agreed," I said. "What are your plans for when we go back to Seattle? You don't have to go back tomorrow, do you? I'd like to stay here for a few days to see if we can exonerate Ray."

Jonah shook his head. "I don't have to be back right away. I do have a few projects to work on, but the deadline for those is next month."

Brandi tugged on a curl. "I haven't built up my client base yet, so I'm good for a few days. But when we get back, I need to go through my list of contacts and make some calls."

"And set up your website," Jonah added. "I can help you with that."

Brandi smiled. "Thank you. I feel a little better just thinking about how I can grow my business, you know what I mean? It's the first time I've been totally responsible for my own success... or failure."

"You won't fail." I leaned forward. "You're driven. You can make it happen."

"What about you, Clarity?" Jonah nudged me. "What are your next steps for your business?"

I watched a moth flutter to the light near the door to the kitchen. "Well, I submitted my application for a private investigator's license."

"Good." Brandi swiped at a mosquito. "When will you get it?"

I shrugged. "Not sure. But the application said it can take up to three weeks."

"That's a long time to wait," Jonah said.

"It will feel like forever. But in the meantime, I'm going to do some freelance marketing to help pay the bills."

"I'm sure I have a few clients that could use some marketing or social media work." Jonah took off his glasses and rubbed his eyes. "All that cider made me tired. I think I'll go to bed."

I yawned. "Me too."

Brandi checked the time on her phone. "Wow. It's already after eleven o'clock. I'd better get some sleep too."

On the way to my room, my phone buzzed. It was a text from a number I didn't recognize.

"You disappointed me tonight. No one has ever told me no. It excites me," the text read.

"Oh, my God." It was from Nathan. That man was seriously sick. I needed to show this to someone.

Knocking softly on Hunter's door and then Zen's, I waited for them to answer. I knocked again, a little louder this time.

Hunter appeared in the doorway of the room next to Zen's. "Clarity. What's wrong?"

I showed him the text.

His eyes darkened, and his jaw flexed. "Zen and I will have a talk with him tomorrow."

Zen opened his door, his normally perfect hair disheveled from sleep. "What's going on?"

Just as I showed him the text, another one came through. "I'll pick you up at six tomorrow night. Wear something sexy."

Zen narrowed his eyes. "That is not going to happen."

"Duh." I stared at the screen in disbelief. "Who does he think he is?"

"Tell you what." Hunter stepped closer to Zen. "We'll all meet up with him at six tomorrow. I think he'll get the idea he needs to stay the hell away from you."

Zen grinned. "I think we can get the message across quite clearly."

"I know guys like that. He'll need a fresh change of underwear before we're finished with him." The corners of Hunter's lips turned up and his dimples appeared for the first time today.

The aggressive bro talk seemed to smooth over their previous tension.

"Wait!" Alarm squeezed my chest tight. "You're not going to beat him up, are you?"

"No, of course not." Zen crossed his arms.

"Good." I smiled. "Because I was hoping I'd get the chance to do that."

Hunter laughed. "I guess it's a good thing Zen and I will be there to protect him."

I snorted. "Just give me five minutes alone with him first."

"In all seriousness," Zen said, "this will give us a good chance to interview Dr. Strong about Arnold. Maybe this nefarious doctor had something to do with Arnold's death."

Hunter agreed. "Seems likely, now that we know more about his true character."

That gave me pause. Maybe Nathan wasn't just a misogynistic womanizer.

Maybe he was a killer.

CHAPTER 24

I was the first one up.

Mom had fixed French toast in the morning. Whipped cream, fresh berries, and huckleberry syrup were set out on the countertop. My stomach grumbled, and I could actually feel the drool about to escape the corners of my mouth.

"Mom, this looks amazing."

"Thanks, honey. Help yourself and let me know if you want or need anything else."

"You're the best. Thanks."

Today, she was wearing threadbare jeans and a bright yellow and blue tie-dyed shirt. Her dark braid was graying and frayed at the ends. I wondered how long it had been since she'd had a haircut. If she'd let me, I'd treat her to a day of pampering.

"Mom, what are you doing today?" I loaded my plate with two slices of French toast and piled on the toppings.

"Oh, the usual." She plugged in the coffeemaker and spooned some freshly ground coffee beans into the basket. It smelled divine.

"What's the usual?" I sat at the table and took a bite.

"Gotta feed the chickens, collect eggs, feed the goats and milk them, then start a batch of cider."

"If I can get my friends to do those chores, will you come with me on a little outing?"

She raised her eyebrows. "An outing? Where to?"

"It's a surprise." I grinned and shoveled a big mouthful of food into my mouth.

"I'm not sure I like that. The last time I was surprised is when the goats demolished our marijuana crop."

I laughed, accidentally blowing a blob of whipped cream onto the table. "Oops." I wiped it up with a napkin. "It's not that kind of surprise, I guarantee it."

She wrinkled her nose. "I don't know. Those goats aren't easy to milk. I don't know what they'll do if two strangers tried to put their hands on their teats."

"Oh, I'm sure they'll be fine. Dad will be there to supervise."

She shrugged. "Right on. I'm up for it."

Brandi and Jonah came into the kitchen just as the coffee pot finished percolating.

"This looks yummy." Brandi grabbed a plate. "Jonah, you first."

He helped himself to a big helping of food.

"Coffee, anyone?" Mom got out a few mugs.

"Yes, please," we said in unison.

"Coming right up." Cream and sugar are on the table."

"Mom, since when do you make coffee? I thought you were going to make those awful wheatgrass smoothies." I licked the whipped cream off my fork.

She smiled. "When I have guests, I serve coffee. For some reason, no one but me likes the wheatgrass smoothies."

"To each his or her own, I guess." Jonah opened a cabinet door, looking for a coffee cup.

"Guys." I got up to get a mug out of the cabinet. "Would you be willing to do some of the farm chores this morning so I can treat my mom to a few hours of relaxation?"

Jonah shrugged. "Sure, why not? As long as someone shows us how."

Brandi fixed her cup of coffee. "Honestly, I'd love that. It will take my mind off what's going on with Ray."

"Great. After we eat, Dad can show you what to do while I take Mom out on the town."

✳✳✳

Since I'd started a new business, I was supposed to be saving money. But I wanted to do something special for Mom. She spent her days chasing goats, working in the garden, making cider, among many other tasks and chores. She deserved to be pampered.

"First stop is Salon Magnifique." I brought Dad's truck to a rumbling halt in front of the business. "I called ahead and made you an appointment." I didn't tell her how much it would cost.

"A haircut?" Mom shook her head in wonder. "I haven't had a haircut since 1986."

My mouth hung open. "Seriously? Aren't you worried about split ends?"

"Hell, no." Mom opened the truck door. "I just chop off the end of my braid with kitchen scissors every now and then. Works just fine."

I climbed out of the truck and wrenched the door shut behind me. "Well, let's see if you like what they do better."

The inside of the salon smelled like expensive shampoo and nail polish. Nondescript music played softly in the background.

"May I help you?" A woman looking overly styled and made-up beamed as we approached the counter. She took in my farm fresh appearance and Mom's graying braid and tie-dye shirt. Her enthusiasm faltered.

"Yes." I smiled brightly. "My mom has an appointment with Jacques. I pointed at her name on the list. "Her name is Wanda Bloom. And I'm Clarity. I have a nail appointment with Deborah."

"You mean Deborah?" She pronounced it Debohra with the emphasis on the "bohr".

"Uh, sure." I glanced at Mom. She bit her lip, trying hard not to laugh.

"All right ladies, we'll get you started." She gave Mom a disapproving look. "Please put on a robe and then meet us back here."

"A robe?" Mom was clearly out of her element. "Is this like a daytime sleepover kind of thing?"

I grinned. "No. They have you put on a robe so they don't get hair dye or stray hairs all over your clothing."

Mom shrugged. "Okay. Whatever you say."

Jacques was waiting for us by his station. "Welcome, madame et mademoiselle!" He rushed toward us and kissed each of us on both cheeks.

Mom giggled. "He's so fancy. Is he French?" she whispered.

I smiled. "Probably."

Mom sat in the chair and looked into the mirror. For the first time ever, I saw the disappointment in her eyes.

"I guess I haven't taken very good care of myself."

"Nonsense." Jacques began playing with her braid. "You are a natural beauty. I can tell your spirit is pure. You must do very much for everyone else, yes?"

Mom nodded. "I guess so."

"Well, now it is time for you to do something for you."

Mom's eyes were glassy. I reached out and squeezed her hand. "You deserve it."

Jacques unbraided her dark, graying braid and gasped at how long it was. "Mon Dieu! This is incroyable!"

Her hair cascaded down her back in waves. It reached the seat cushion. I put my hand to my mouth. It was much longer than I'd guessed. "Wow, Mom. That's a lot of hair."

She wiped away a tear and nodded.

"Oh, madame, I will make you look amazing. I guarantee it." He looked at her reflection for a bit, cocked his head to one side, and then asked, "Tell me about your everyday life. What is it that you do?"

Mom glanced at all the women waiting in the salon's seating area. They already looked put-together and fashionable—and they hadn't even had their services done yet.

She cleared her throat. "Well, Darren and I have a bed and breakfast that we run."

"Oh, very nice!" The man held up the ends of her hair and inspected them.

"And we have an apple orchard. We make cider. And we have goats and chickens—and a garden."

I thought to myself, please don't mention the marijuana crop, please, please.

"And we grow some pretty high-grade weed."

I put my hand to my forehead.

Jacques' eyebrows rose up into his forehead, creating creases that hadn't been there before. "I was not expecting that." He chuckled. "A pleasant surprise, for sure."

Soon, they were talking about CBD oil and all the products you could make from hemp.

I checked the time. My nail appointment was in just a few minutes. I had just enough time to go to the bathroom.

On my way there, I walked past a tall woman with her head under a dryer, reading a magazine. Sections of her blond hair were wrapped in foil. Was that who I thought it was?

She looked up from her magazine. Shoot! I desperately looked around for a place to hide. There was a door not too far from where I stood. With one last look over my shoulder, I grasped the knob, gave it a twist, and slipped inside.

Two startled aestheticians looked up from their customer, who was buck naked from the waist down awaiting her Brazilian wax.

My face drained of color and my breath caught in my throat. Oh. My. God.

The waxee let out a high-pitched squeal. "Get out!"

"I'm so sorry!" I squeaked. Before they could say another word, I felt for the doorknob behind me, wrenched it open, and then closed it in a fraction of a second. Sweat poured off me and I hitched in a panicked breath. The term "mortification" didn't even begin to touch how I felt.

The sounds of hysterical rambling accompanied by the soothing sounds of the aestheticians' voices trying to calm down their customer came through the door, followed by the click of the lock.

That poor woman. She would forever be traumatized by this incident. And so would I.

After my heart stopped racing, I checked to see if Astrid had seen me emerge from the door. I breathed a sigh of relief when I saw that her head was down, her attention riveted on a magazine.

With a sigh of relief, I escaped my hiding spot and made my way to the bathroom, did my business, and snuck back to where Astrid was sitting. She was still under the dryer, but she now had her cell phone to her ear and was totally immersed in a conversation with whomever was on the other end. Her foil-wrapped hair concealed her view of me this time, so I focused on what she was saying.

"The police told me not to leave town."

I gasped and tried to blend into the wall.

She listened a moment. "Yes, I know they've arrested Ray, but they never told me I was free to go." Pause. "Right. I'll meet you there."

I knew it! Astrid was somehow involved in Arnold's death. I'd witnessed some suspicious behavior from her in the last few days. There was no way I would let Ray take the fall for Astrid's crime. But how could I prove it?

The nail technician appeared in the doorway in the wall. "Clarity?"

I smiled. "That's me." I glanced over at Astrid to see if she'd heard my name, but the dryer was loud, and she was reading something on her phone.

There was just enough time for Mom to get her hair styled and for me to get my nails done. Then we would follow Astrid to wherever she was going.

Anger fueled my adrenaline. I breathed out hard. I needed to find out if she'd killed Arnold.

CHAPTER 25

"Mom, you look beautiful!" I stared at her reflection in the stylist's mirror. Her long graying hair had been expertly cut to shoulder length, with long layers, giving it volume and a nice shape. It had been transformed back to her natural dark color with a few highlights to frame her face.

Jacques had applied minimal makeup to enhance her natural beauty. It was just the right amount and made her look more vibrant. It suddenly hit me that I looked a lot like her.

Mom blinked away tears. "Is that me?"

I leaned over and hugged her from behind. "It's you. You've always been beautiful. You just take care of everyone else all the time. Maybe you should start caring for yourself a little, too."

Mom nodded. "Right on. Thank you, sweet girl."

My attention shifted to the tall blonde who'd made her way to the counter to pay her bill. Her hair was perfectly styled in long beachy waves. Everyone in the shop gawked at her, trying to figure out if she was someone famous. She seemed distracted enough to not notice them or me, for that matter.

It was time for action.

I turned back to Jacques. "Thank you so much for making my mom as beautiful on the outside as she is on the inside." I gave him a hug and nudged Mom to get up. "How much do we owe you?"

We settled up at the counter just as the glass door swung closed behind Astrid. Seconds later, I watched her drive by in a sleek black car.

"Let's go." I whisked Mom out the door and hurried to her truck.

Mom gave me a confused look "What's the hurry?"

"See that woman in the rental car ahead of us?" I pointed at the black sedan. "I think she may have been involved in the death of Ray's cousin."

"What? That super model chick killed someone?"

"She's actually an Olympic athlete. I don't know for certain that she killed Arnold, but I'm determined to find out."

"This is more exciting than chasing the goats away from Farmer Ned's raspberry bushes!" Mom grinned and pointed to the gas pedal on the truck. "Step on it."

I pushed my foot down on the stiff pedal. I had my doubts as to whether or not the old Ford truck could keep up with Astrid's Audi, but I was about to find out.

Astrid sped ahead, turning right just as the traffic light turned red.

"Shoot." I stopped and looked to see if cars were coming. I had just enough time to turn before the next wave of traffic. I floored it and tried to avoid a lamp post.

"That's right, sweetie! Pedal to the metal!" Mom whooped.

I did my best to keep up with Astrid's Audi without being obvious. Where was she headed? Back to her hotel?

Astrid turned left at a four-way stop, onto a backroad that paralleled the freeway. There were no other cars on that stretch. Surely, she'd notice if we followed.

I brought the truck to a stop, watching her continue on the straight road. I could still see her, so when it was my turn to go, I turned left and followed slowly.

"Go, go, go!" Mom pumped her fist.

"Not so fast. I don't want her to notice we're following her." I drove at a steady pace.

Mom gripped my shoulder. "What if we go faster and pass her? Then we can torque the wheel and block the road so she can't get away!"

I turned to glance at my mom. Who was this person sitting next to me? "No! I don't want her to T-bone the truck. She'll kill us!"

"Oh, honey. This truck is made of good ol' American steel. It's like a tank. Go ahead and do it. Dad can get another farm truck. We'll just add another half-acre crop of weed to pay for it."

"Mom, no! That's crazy." I checked the rearview mirror. No cops and no other cars. "Besides, I just want to know where she's going."

Mom looked deflated. "Well, all right. But don't blame me if she gets away."

The road was straight for a good mile or so. I had no problem keeping Astrid's car in my line of sight. But up ahead, the road bent in a large curve and trees sprung up on either side of the pavement. Visibility would be limited once we entered the curve. I sped up a little to close the distance between our vehicles.

Astrid's car suddenly accelerated. Had she seen us behind her?

I chewed on my lip, debating if I should go faster or if I should continue to hang back and try to be less conspicuous.

Mom grabbed the handle on the roof near her window that our family affectionately dubbed the "oh, shit bar." She glanced at me expectantly.

"Well," she said, "what are you waiting for? Gun it!"

The debate in my mind was over. I needed to speed up or risk losing Astrid. My foot stomped down on the gas. The old truck grumbled and made a whining noise.

"Come on! Burn rubber!" Mom hooted, leaning forward in her seat.

I peeked at the speedometer. We were up to sixty-eight miles per hour. Could the truck go any faster?

Astrid took the corner up ahead at a breakneck speed.

"She's getting away!" Mom screeched.

"I'm trying." The truck began to shudder as I pushed the gas pedal down as far as it would go. Now we were up to seventy-three miles per hour.

There wasn't just one curve up ahead. The road snaked in a series of curves. I knew we wouldn't be able to keep up with Astrid's Audi, especially the way the truck's tires were squealing in the turns.

"Try harder," Mom growled. "We'll lose her."

The truck was operating at its maximum speed of seventy-five miles per hour. I knew it had hit its limit because the rattling noise coming from underneath was deafening.

"Mom, I don't think—"

Before I could finish my sentence, a large spotted cow appeared on the winding road, less than a hundred yards away. It sauntered to the middle of the narrow road and turned to watch us race toward it. I hitched in a breath and slammed on the brakes, sending Mom and me lunging forward against the constraint of our seatbelts.

We slid, tires screeching, off to the left. I corrected, and we slid back to the right. The back of the truck fishtailed wildly. We stopped just a few feet away from the animal, who stared at us with her big brown eyes.

I coughed and put my hand to my chest where the seatbelt had dug into my skin. "Ouch."

Mom grimaced and watched the cow cross the road. "Dang thing must've gotten away from some farm."

"Are you all right, Mom?" I glanced sideways at her. She seemed completely calm. At least, she seemed a lot calmer than I felt.

"I'm fine. Hang on." She jumped out of the truck and approached the cow and spoke to her in low tones.

I rolled down the window so I could hear what she was saying.

"Easy girl. Where did you come from?" She stroked the cow's back and inspected her flank. "You've got the Starlight Ranch brand stamped on you. Poor girl. Tell you what—I'll come back with the trailer for you. If you're still here, I'll take you somewhere safe."

Mom gave the cow one more pat and then jumped back into the truck. "Best to get going before the fuzz comes. We need to catch up with the super model."

I shook my head and put the truck into gear, gently pushing down on the gas pedal. "I don't think 'the fuzz' is after us quite yet, but they will be if we keep going as fast as we just were." I glanced at Mom. "I don't think this old truck can take much more. How old is this thing, anyway?"

Mom scrunched her eyebrows together. "I don't know. At least as old as you."

Once we were rolling again, we passed through several more curves, with Astrid nowhere in sight.

"Well, we lost her." Mom crossed her arms.

I swallowed a giggle. She was full-on pouting. I'd never seen her like this before. Where had this need for speed and getting the bad guy come from?

The road straightened out again, and it was starting to look kind of familiar. Was this the road to the—

"Casino!" Mom shouted.

Sure enough, up ahead was the Skagit River Casino sign. And just pulling into its parking lot, was a shiny black Audi.

CHAPTER 26

The truck rumbled to a stop in the space opposite Astrid's car. Mom wrenched the door open and flung herself out of the vehicle.

"Mom, wait!" I unbuckled my seatbelt and shouldered the door open. "You can't just bust in there. We need some kind of plan."

"Plan?" Mom looked like she was going to sprint for the entrance.

"Yeah, a plan." I resisted the urge to roll my eyes. "What are we going to say to her after we storm the castle?"

Mom stopped for a moment, her face blank. "I don't know. I guess we tell her she killed what's-his-face's brother."

I put my hand on her arm. "First of all, we don't know that she killed anybody. But what's his face is Ray. And what's-his-face's brother isn't his brother, it's his cousin."

"Oh." She didn't care. There was a gleam of adventure in her eyes. She was ready to storm into the casino.

"Give me a moment to think." I stared at the nearby trees and chewed on my lip.

After a few minutes, I said, "Astrid knows who I am, but she doesn't know who you are."

Mom shrugged. "True."

"Do you have your cell phone with you?"

"My phone?" She pulled it out of her back pocket. "Yep, it's right here."

"Good." I took it from her and called my cell. When my phone rang, I accepted the call. "Now we're connected. I can listen in if you talk to her—which you should avoid, by the way. Just go in and see who she's meeting. Have your phone out so you can take a picture of her and whoever she's talking to. Got it?"

Mom frowned. "I can't confront her, then?"

My shoulders sagged. "No. Do not do that. She's dangerous. If you get into trouble, say '911', and I'll come in after you, okay?"

The look of disappointment etched Mom's lines around her mouth, making her look older than she was.

To perk her up, I said, "Pretend you're one of those spy ladies from the 007 movies you love so much. Be cool and sneaky."

Mom's eyes brightened. "Like Pussy Galore?"

Good Lord. "Is she a spy lady from one of the 007 movies?"

"Hell, yeah. She's a badass villainess from Goldfinger." Mom's sly smile spread across her face.

"Okay. Be her. But instead of a villainess, be the heroine." I pointed to the casino. "Go get 'em, Pussy."

Mom got halfway to the door before she turned around and jogged back to the truck. "Clarity, I can't go in there looking like this!" She looked down at her tie-dye t-shirt. "Pussy would never wear this."

197

I gritted my teeth, knowing I had to appease her if I wanted her to get this right. I dug the credit card out of my purse. "Here. There's a little boutique shop to the left as you enter. Try not to spend too much. I'm on a budget."

"Right on." Mom trotted off to the entrance and disappeared through the dark tinted glass doors of the casino.

I stared out the window and listened on the open cell phone line as Mom searched for an outfit. She wasn't much of a shopper. It didn't take long before she was at the cash register paying for her disguise. Now she was on the hunt for Astrid.

Mom's voice came through my phone. "Clarity, I've exited the boutique. I'm covering the southwest quadrant, surveilling the slot machines. Over."

I rolled my eyes. "Okay, check the poker tables. Seems more like Astrid's speed."

"Roger that."

I heard rustling sounds as my mother swished through the casino.

"Bingo room, all clear."

"Good. Have you gotten to the poker tables yet?" I stared out the window at the clouds floating by.

"Ten-four. Approaching the area now."

Finally. I had a momentary bout of panic when I thought about my mom possibly confronting the tall, strong Olympian. I just hoped Astrid wasn't into beating up older ladies. Although, I was pretty sure after years of farming, wrestling goats, and what not, Mom would be a formidable opponent.

"Suspect spotted ahead," Mom whispered into the phone.

I sat up straight. "Where?"

"In the hallway leading to the restrooms."

"Is she with anyone?"

"Affirmative. Tall man wearing baseball cap."

That had to be Carlson. "Does he have dark hair?"

"Can't tell, Clarity."

"Shh, Mom! Don't use my name and don't talk so loud." I gritted my teeth.

Mom's voice snaked through the line. "Sorry. I'll have to get closer to see if he has any identifying features. Over."

"Be careful." I groaned. She was going to mess this up. I only hoped she could make a quick exit before Astrid got a hold of her.

Boop! A series of tones followed the first one.

"Mom?"

Beep, boop, boop.

"Mom? Are you there?" I held the phone out to see if we were still connected.

"Shoot. Sorry. I stuck the phone in my waistband for a second. These leggings don't have pockets. I'm trying to find a hiding spot behind a plant."

"I won't be able to hear anything if you put your phone in your pants. Just keep it in your hand, okay?" I sighed and waited while she got into her hiding place.

"Tall man and super model are arguing," Mom whispered. "Her face is all red and she looks like she's ready to slug him."

My interest was piqued. "Can you hear what they're saying?"

"Oh! There's another guy with a hat joining them. He's tall too."

Other guy? "Mom, what does he look like?"

"They're arguing. Oooh! It's getting interesting! I'm going to take some pictures."

"What are they saying?"

Beep, boop.

"Mom?" I waited. "Mom?"

The line went dead.

Crap. I waited a second and then jabbed redial. "Come on, answer." I leaned forward, waiting for her to come out of the front doors.

I stared at the phone, willing her to answer the call. But it rang through to voice mail. I ended the call. There was no choice. I had to go after her.

Wrenching the truck door open, I slammed it behind me and ran for the entrance. Just as I reached for the door grip, it flew open, the force of it nearly knocking me backward.

A woman sprinted past me into the parking lot. She was running, despite the fact her 3-inch vinyl stilettos were clearly something she wasn't used to walking—let alone—running in. Her skinny chicken legs were clothed in tight leopard print leggings. Her black, sparkling tube top inched its way down her back as she hobbled toward my dad's truck. My dad's truck...

Was that?

"Mom?"

My mother barely turned her head as she yelled. "What the hell are you waiting for? Let's get out of here!"

I ran, not knowing why I was running.

The casino doors exploded open behind me. Without turning my head to look, I jumped into the truck, started the engine, and rumbled toward the exit.

In the rearview mirror, I saw three casino security officers bent over, huffing, their faces red and angry.

"Faster!" Mom yelled at me as the truck rumbled out of the parking lot. "Before they send the fuzz after us!"

"The fuzz? Mom, what did you do?"

I jammed my foot down on the gas pedal and felt it sink to the bottom as we hit our maximum speed of sixty miles per hour. The truck made a wheezing noise but continued on.

She twisted around to look through the back window. "Hot damn! We got away. No one is following us."

"Mom—what happened?" Just in case, I searched for a less obvious way home. I turned onto a side road.

Her eyes twinkled. "I got a little too close to those people and that super model chick got suspicious. When she stormed over to me, I thought she was going to throw a punch."

"What did you do?"

"I grabbed the drink out of some loser's hand and threw it at her. But not just the drink—the glass too. I think I may have busted her nose."

My mouth hung open, astonished that she'd lived to tell the tale. No wonder the security guards had chased her.

Mom let out a nervous giggle. "I didn't mean to hurt her. It was a reflex. She was coming at me fast and she's huge! But you should've seen her face. She looked like a drowned rat. Well, a pretty drowned rat with a red nose—but still, a rat."

I laugh escaped my lips. It started out as a chuckle but swelled to a guffaw. And soon, both Mom and I were laughing so hard that tears flowed down our cheeks.

When I finally regained control, I wiped my eyes. "We've got to get serious. I want to know everything that happened."

CHAPTER 27

The truck came to a rumbling halt behind Zen and Hunter's unmarked sedan.

As I got out and slammed the door, two puppies came running toward me, ears flapping and tails wagging.

"Hello there!" I sat down in the dirt and let them crawl into my lap, laughing as they covered my face with wet kisses.

Mom pushed her door open, scrambled out of the truck, and swore under her breath.

My heart jumped. "What's wrong? Are the casino guards coming?"

"No." Mom stood on her wobbling three-inch heels. "I left my old clothes back in the dressing room of the gift shop. After all the hoopla, I couldn't go back and get them."

She looked down at her new duds. "I can't do farm chores in these."

Dad emerged from behind the garden fence. "Clarity! I thought you took your mother somewhere. Where is she?"

He caught sight of Mom, who'd put an unsteady hand on the truck for balance.

"Who's your friend?"

Mom grinned and flipped her hair off her shoulder. "It's me, old man."

Dad squinted his eyes before reaching into his shirt pocket for his glasses. He stared hard at Mom. His eyebrows shot up. "Wanda? Is that you?"

She attempted a sexy catwalk toward him, but her heels sank into the patchy grass alongside the driveway, causing her to yank her feet up and out of the dirt with each step. Undeterred, she purred, "Call me Pussy. Pussy Galore."

Dad's jaw dropped. "Va-va-voom!"

Yuck. I didn't need to see this. I picked up the puppies and got to my feet. "I'll leave you two super spies alone. I'm going to go talk to Zen and Hunter. Mom, join us when you have a moment."

I carried the wriggling puppies toward the front door. Before I could reach it, an ear-piercing shriek split the air. The little dogs howled and pressed their noses into my neck and shook with fright.

"What the—?"

Brandi came tearing around the corner of the house, covered in what looked like mud.

"Look out!" She screamed as she ran past me. The smell of manure lingered in her wake.

Mom and Dad separated from their lip-lock.

"Why is she flippin' out?" Dad watched Brandi scramble up a nearby apple tree.

Jonah suddenly tore around the corner of the house, his shirt dirty and torn. "Run!" He vaulted into the air, grabbed a branch in the tree next to Brandi's, and hoisted himself up.

I stood like a possum caught in headlights, not knowing where to turn or why.

Before I could say or do anything, the sound of pounding hooves and bleating goats exploded from behind the house. My eyes widened as a herd of deranged animals came barreling toward me.

"Not again!" I had a momentary flashback of my ladder accident and forthcoming concussion.

Directly behind the goats was an even larger herd of pigs. Wait, pigs? No, hogs. My parents didn't own hogs. These things were ginormous. My brain churned wildly, trying to process what was happening.

"Clarity!" Hunter burst out of the front door of the house, looking almost as alarmed as I felt. In a heartbeat, he hurdled toward me, sweeping me out of harm's way seconds before the animals pounded past us. Still clutching the puppies to my chest, I gasped as he set me on my feet near an apple tree.

"Are you all right?" He slid his hands to my shoulders and scanned me for injuries.

Breathing hard, I watched the cloud of dust follow the stampeding animals as they ran toward an open field. I tried desperately to calm my wildly beating heart. "I'm fine, I think." My hands shook as I passed him the red puppy. "Take Comet. Can we go inside where it's safe?"

Zen appeared in the open doorway. "What was that noise?"

Dad was in a tizzy. "That danged neighbor! His hogs got out again! That's the third time this month those monsters have terrorized our poor goats."

Mom teetered over to the riding mower and climbed onto the seat. "I'll go over there and give that Jimbo a piece of my mind."

Dad hopped in the truck and rolled down the window. "Stay here, Wanda. I got this. You'll mess up your sexy new clothes if you get into it with that scumbag. I'll handle it." He started the truck, backed up, and peeled away.

I watched the tires kick up gravel in its wake. "Wow. That was dramatic."

"Yeah." Zen turned to look at our mother, taking in her leopard print leggings and tube top. "Mom?"

She grinned and fluffed her hair. "Like the new me?"

Zen's mouth hung open. For once, he was speechless.

I stifled a laugh, but decided I needed to get back to business. "I want to see the pictures you took on your phone." I motioned for her to join us. "The ones you took at the casino."

Zen frowned. "What did you two do? And why is Mom dressed like that?"

I explained the whole thing and watched both Zen and Hunter's expressions turn sour.

"What were you thinking?" Zen fumed. "You could've gotten yourself hurt—and you put Mom at risk."

Mom tutted. "Nonsense. We were fine. Clarity's a real smart girl. She warned me to be careful. I agreed to take the risk. So, if you want to yell at somebody, yell at me."

Zen sighed. "Okay, fine. Let's see the photos you took."

Mom grinned. "Oh, I got some good ones. I think you'll be pleased." She tapped on her camera icon and opened the photos.

Zen took it from her and swiped through the pictures. He groaned. "Mom. You took pictures of yourself."

Mom huffed. "What? No! I took pictures of that amazon super model and the two guys she was arguing with." She snatched the phone away and stared at the pictures.

I peeked over her shoulder. Somehow, Mom had hit the selfie button while she was in Pussy Galore mode. Each photo was a blurred close-up of her face. Her eyes were focused and intent in the first one and panicked and surprised in the last one.

"Nice work," I grumbled.

Mom stayed silent for a few seconds after realizing her blunder. Then she shrugged. "Well, at least I captured some pictures of myself looking hot. I'll try not to make the same mistake next time."

"There won't be a next time," Zen growled. "Your days as a private eye are over."

Mom frowned. "International spy, not private eye. And I'll spy if I want to. You're not the boss of me, young man. Don't forget—I'm still your mother."

I could tell Zen was showing great restraint by biting his tongue, but I could see his jaw clenching. There was no way he would win against Mom.

Instead, he cleared his throat. "Hunter and I are going to do a follow-up interview with this Astrid woman. We'll be back in time to pick you up for our interview with Dr. Strong at six o'clock." He glanced at his partner. "We've got Astrid's number. Call her and let's go."

"Can we come?" Mom grabbed onto my arm and stepped closer to Zen.

"No." Zen climbed into the driver's side of his unmarked police car. Hunter passed his puppy to me and hopped into the passenger side. We watched them drive down the narrow lane toward the main road.

"Help." A small voice came from up high.

I looked up at the trees and saw Brandi perched up on a branch at least fifteen feet above the ground. I'd forgotten all about her.

Jonah, in the next tree over, wasn't nearly as high. He climbed down carefully, hugging the trunk as he scooted down.

"I'll catch you, Brandi," Jonah called up to her. "Jump!"

"Yeah, right." Brandi shook her head. "I'm not doing that."

I set the puppy down and ran to grab a ladder. It was only a few rows of apple trees into the orchard.

"Here." I set the ladder underneath where Brandi was hugging a branch. "Just shimmy down a bit and put your foot on the top. Jonah and I will help you."

With reluctance, Brandi did as I'd instructed and soon she was standing next to us.

I took in my friends' disheveled appearances. Brandi had splotches of dirt across her cheeks. Her curly hair was popping out of the ponytail holder and was encrusted with something brown. I hoped it was mud, but it smelled suspiciously like manure. Her knees were dirty and scraped, tiny rocks sticking to her torn flesh.

Jonah was in a similar condition, with the added bonus of having his T-shirt torn in several places.

"What happened to you guys? Why were those hogs chasing you and the goats?" I asked.

Brandi scowled. "We were trying to milk the goats, but they weren't having it. They kicked at us and got away somehow. We ran after them to the back fence."

Jonah wiped the dirt off his forehead. "Yeah, and when we ran toward them, the hogs on the other side of the fence got really mean. They charged us and busted through the fencing and attacked us."

I tried hard not to laugh. "That sounds awful. How did you get that, uh, dirt all over you?" I pointed to the smears of brown covering my friends' skin and clothing. The distinct odor of animal dung floated fragrantly in the air.

Brandi frowned. "It started with the goats. Apparently, they don't like to be milked by strangers. Their little hooves are dirty, and after they kicked us multiple times, we realized that the dirt wasn't really dirt."

"I guess we should've mucked out their stalls before we milked them, like your mom advised." Jonah gave Mom a nervous glance.

Mom said nothing, but her self-satisfied grin said it all.

"You got all that poop on you from the goats?" I asked.

Brandi groaned. "No. There are big piles of it near the fence that borders the neighbors hog pen. Judging by the size of the poo, my guess is that the hogs have marked the property as theirs."

"Yeah." Jonah frowned. "We must've tripped and fallen in it at least a dozen times while we were trying to escape them."

Mom shook her head. "Those damn hogs. I think we're going to have to electrify our fence."

"Probably a good idea." I glanced at the road. "Let's go inside before the herd of hogs decides to come back."

We took the puppies inside the house.

"Brandi and Jonah," Mom said, "why don't you go wash up and put on some clean clothes while I get you a snack and something to drink. Is lemonade okay?"

Jonah hesitated. "I could use something a little stronger than lemonade, if that's all right."

"Me too." Brandi brushed a loose curl from her smudged forehead. "It's been a day."

"I got you covered. Zen bought beer. It's in the fridge." Mom went into the kitchen and busied herself with preparing a snack and drinks.

"Need some help?" I asked.

"No. You just keep those pups occupied so they don't come in the kitchen."

I played with the little fur sharks until Brandi and Jonah showed up, looking much cleaner. They smelled better too.

"Wow." Brandi opened a beer and took a sip. "I'm curious about what Astrid was up to, meeting in the casino like that. And who were those men with her?"

"And to be so hostile toward Wanda when they discovered she was taking photos of them." Jonah gently removed Kodiak away from his shoelaces and placed him on his lap. "They're hiding something."

"Do you know who the men were, Wanda? Did they mention names or anything?" Brandi asked.

Mom shook her head. "Nope. I couldn't hear what they were saying until they came after me."

"What did they look like?" Jonah spotted Pumpkin sauntering into the room and held out his hand to pet him.

Mom shrugged. "They were tall. That's all I know. They were both wearing baseball caps and sunglasses."

"Any facial hair?" I asked.

"I can't remember." Mom reached into the fridge and pulled out some apples. She sliced them and arranged them on a plate with a cup of peanut butter drizzled with honey.

"Yum." I took the plate from her and set it on the dining table.

Brandi and Jonah shooed the puppies away toward the open kitchen door.

"I wonder if Zen and Hunter found Astrid?" I said. "I'll text them."

Seconds later, Hunter returned my text. "Astrid is MIA. She's not answering her phone. We checked the hotel where she's staying, and she's not here."

"Shoot," I said, turning to Brandi and Jonah. "They can't find Astrid."

"Supermodel made a getaway, huh?" Mom smirked. "I knew she was a bad egg."

"Where do you think she went?" Brandi asked.

I stared out the window, thinking. "Let's talk this through. If Astrid was at the casino with two tall men, and they were having a heated discussion…"

Jonah sat up straight. "The tall men could've been Carlson and—who else in our rafting group was tall?"

I frowned. "There were a few tall men in the other groups, but Astrid didn't seem to know them."

"What about Joe?" Brandi asked.

"Joe? The older gentleman who sat at our table for dinner at The Black Swan?" I said. "He's a nice guy. But he didn't seem too close with Astrid or the others."

Brandi shrugged. "He's the only other tall guy who was friendly with Astrid. I don't know who else it could be."

"Okay, then, let's say it was Joe. What in the world would they be meeting about?" I said.

"Didn't you say that Joe told you that Arnold tried to start his own adventure travel company and it didn't do very well?" Jonah asked.

I nodded. "Yeah. He mentioned that." I thought about my conversation with Joe at The Black Swan. "I got the idea that he wasn't a huge fan of Arnold. He wasn't that impressed with him. But he was a big fan of Ray's. That's why he's been on multiple excursions with Ray's company."

"Was there a connection between Astrid and Joe?" Brand sipped her beer.

"Not that I could tell." I got up and stretched. "None of this is making sense. I almost feel like if we go back to the place where Arnold's body was found, maybe we'll find some clues."

"Then, let's do it!" Mom stood with her feet planted apart, like she was ready to take on the world.

I laughed. "Mom, come on. The police have already combed through that area. I don't think it's a good idea."

"Why not?" Jonah got up and moved to Mom's side. "What do we have to lose?"

Brandi grinned. "Yeah, I'm up for it."

"It'll take at least a half hour to drive there." I looked at each of their hopeful faces and caved. "Oh, all right. But I'm texting Hunter and Zen to let them know where we're going. Just in case."

Mom grinned. "Hot damn. Let's go!"

Dad came in through the back door just as we were going out the front. "Hey, where are you guys all going?"

"We're gonna catch some bad guys." Mom looked down at her tube top, which was beginning to make its way south. "Right after I change into some clothes I can move in—you know, in case the bad guys chase us."

Dad seemed to take this all in stride. "Right on. I'll stay and watch the puppies. Have a good time."

A few minutes later, the four of us were crammed into Jonah's small SUV.

Mom rolled down the window and waved at Dad. "Don't forget to collect the chicken eggs! I want to make a lemon meringue pie when we get back."

Dad nodded. "Any chance I can get you to put that new outfit on after the kids have gone to bed?"

Mom hooted. "Hell, yeah!"

I shuddered. I'm glad my parents still loved each other after all these years, but I didn't want to think about them doing the nasty.

✳✳✳

We drove forty minutes to get to the side road that led to the river. We passed fields of tulips, lavender, mint, and hay.

I sat quietly in the front passenger seat next to Jonah, watching for the narrow drive that led to the site where we'd camped. I ignored the others kidding Mom about her spy adventures and thought about Arnold's murder. Was Astrid the killer? She was certainly strong enough. Had she killed him in anger, or had it been planned? Or perhaps one of the others had killed him.

"Is this where I turn?" Jonah tipped his chin toward an overgrown service road to the right.

"Maybe?" I frowned. How many of these deserted roads were on this stretch? It looked vaguely familiar, but then, so did the last five.

Jonah slowed the vehicle and turned onto the dusty one-lane drive.

"This is the right one!" Brandi pointed to a wooden sign that said: Raft Pick-Up.

"Yeah, I remember seeing that when our van drove us out of here." I craned my neck to catch a last glimpse of the sign. "And I remember that weird tree covered with moss, too."

"Good." Jonah's shoulders relaxed.

Mom leaned forward, the seatbelt straining against her enthusiasm. "Who or what are we looking for again?"

"Astrid." Brandi's eyes focused ahead as she stared out the front window.

"Or maybe something that Astrid left behind." I turned to give Brandi a meaningful look. "Remember we heard her say she lost her gold necklace with the Olympics symbol on it?"

"Right." Jonah hit a pothole and cursed under his breath. "If Astrid killed Arnold, she may have lost the necklace while they fought."

"Except I don't think Arnold knew what was coming. It was clear the killer hit him in the back of the head with a paddle." I spied the turnout for the rafting vans ahead and saw a black car covered with dust from the road. "Wait. Park off the road over there." I pointed to a turnout hidden by a few rhododendron bushes.

"What? Why?" Jonah glanced at me, as he pulled into the hiding place.

"That's Astrid's car up ahead. I don't want her to know we're here." I slipped out of my seatbelt and opened the car door as quietly as I could. "Come on," I whispered.

Jonah and Brandi followed my lead. Mom, however, slunk out of the car as if she were a shadow, hugging the side of the car like she was part of it.

"What are you doing?" I whispered.

She gave me a fierce scowl. "I'm being stealthy. Why don't you give it a try?"

I bit my lip to keep from snickering. "No one is as stealthy as Pussy Galore."

"Damn right." Mom slid alongside the car and then ducked behind a tree.

Grinning, I made eye contact with Brandi and Jonah. "Humor her."

We crept along the sides of the road, hiding behind trees and bushes. Once we reached Astrid's car, I noticed a second vehicle hidden in the brush. It was a dark gray Lexus sedan.

I glanced at Jonah and pointed. He nodded. We had to be cautious. Something was going on, and I didn't want us to be caught in the middle of it. "Stay back," I whispered to Mom and my friends.

Sneaking as quietly as I could toward Astrid's car, I peeked inside. No one was in it. "Clear," I mouthed at my posse. Next, I crept into the brush, where the gray sedan was hidden. Empty.

As soon as I made it back to where my friends were hiding, I heard angry voices coming from the path that led to the river.

I held my breath.

"Damn it! What the hell were you thinking?" a man's voice boomed.

Then a woman's voice... angry, but shaky as well. "You know exactly what I was thinking."

Was that Astrid?

"You two, shut up. We have to find the necklace," another man scolded. "It's probably near where Arnold's body was found. We can't risk the police discovering it."

The voices grew louder, their feet snapping small twigs as they moved toward us. My heart thumped faster in my chest. I motioned for Mom and my friends to stay low and not make a sound.

"Come on," one of the men said. "Let's go back into the woods and check near the campsite."

I didn't dare move or try to catch a glimpse of them. If I could see them, they could see me, and we would be in serious trouble.

When I was sure they couldn't see or hear us, I got up from my crouch. Jonah and Brandi followed suit, but Mom was nowhere to be found.

Panic paralyzed me. Had she gone after them?

"Mom!" I hissed.

"She went that way—toward the river!" Brandi whispered.

Frustration surged through me. She wasn't Pussy Galore. She was a hippie who'd spent her life raising kids and goats. And right now, she was putting herself and us in mortal danger.

"We'll have to go after her," I growled.

"Hurry, before those people come back." Brandi ran ahead, trying not to make noise.

Jonah and I followed.

When we got to the river's edge, I looked up and down the bank. The water was running high and fast. I hoped my mother hadn't fallen in. I didn't know how strong a swimmer she was.

A water bird of some sort lifted off a rock and flapped away. My gaze followed its path for a moment before it settled on an area about hundred feet downstream. Mom stood frozen near a cluster of logs that had caught on some rocks.

She looked up as we approached, her eyes wide and watery. She pointed at the little pool created by the log jam.

A figure was floating face down in the river. Her blond hair drifted out in long tendrils around her head. She reminded me of the character from Hamlet. But this was no Ophelia.

It was Astrid.

CHAPTER 28

"Oh my God," I whispered.

Jonah rushed to Mom's side. "We've got to see if she's still alive. Help me turn her over."

I took a deep breath and joined him as he tried to roll her body nestled among the waterlogged branches.

She was heavy. Her muscular frame weighed her down in the cold water. Jonah and I finally succeeded, and we stared in horror as her blue face turned up to the sky. I lifted her wrist to feel for a pulse. There was no spark of life left in her body.

She was gone.

I stood up. "She's dead. We should leave her right here for the investigators. Let's not contaminate the crime scene any more than we already have. Brandi, see if you can get cell phone signal and call Zen and Hunter."

Mom had backed up during our attempt at turning Astrid over and was now sitting on a rock with her head in her hands.

"You okay, Mom?" I went to her side and rubbed her back.

She sighed. "Yeah. It's just that, Pussy Galore would be fine. She'd just move on to her next mission. But I'm not fine. That woman is dead."

I led her away from the river's edge. "Come on. Let's get you back to the car."

"Got it! Sort of." Brandi waved her phone in the air and then put it to her ear. "Zen, hi. Come quick. We found Astrid. She's dead."

She listened for a moment and then said, "You're breaking up. I can't hear you. We're at the site of Arnold's murder. We found Astrid in the river. Hurry!"

Brandi frowned. "I lost the signal. I don't know if Zen heard a word I said."

I swore under my breath. "We need to go get help."

"Shhh." Mom put a finger to her lips.

The voices we'd heard earlier had come back.

"Let's get out of here," Brandi whispered. "Whoever killed Astrid is coming our way."

"Come on!" I grabbed Mom's hand and tugged her away from the river and back to where the cars were parked. "We need to hide."

We bent down, and single file, we made our way back to the parked vehicles. The voices were getting louder as they got closer, their footsteps now audible over the sound of the river.

Mom stumbled, then froze like a frightened rabbit.

"What's that noise?" The woman's voice said.

The footsteps stopped as the people listened.

We froze behind a large clump of bushes.

"What noise?" One of the men said.

"I heard something moving in the brush," the woman said.

I stared at the pale faces of my mom and my friends. I put my finger to my lips. As quietly as I could, I picked up a large rock in the dirt next to my foot.

"I don't hear anything," one man said. He sounded vaguely familiar…

"I think it came from over here," the woman said. The crunch of her footsteps came toward us.

My heart beat fast. If these people had killed Astrid, they were probably comfortable with killing us as well.

The rock felt heavy in my hand. The footsteps grew closer.

A squirrel chirped.

Without hesitation, I swung my arm back and flung the rock off into the bushes far from where we were hiding.

A squirrel chirped louder and darted up a tree.

One of the men laughed and pointed in the opposite direction of our hideout. "It was just a squirrel. You're being paranoid."

"Paranoid?" There was acid in her voice. "I'm just watching out for us—one of us has to."

"What is that supposed to mean?" the man said.

Her voice was low, but venom dripped from it. "You know what it means. It was your doing that got us into this mess. So, I had to get us out of it."

"Get us out of it?" He almost shouted. "You killed her! Now we have two murders on our hands instead of one."

"Hey, hey," the other man's voice said. "It won't do us any good to fight. Let's be rational. We need to get out of here before anyone else comes along. Two murders are enough. We've got Astrid's necklace. Let's cut our losses and get out of here."

Realization hit me. That was Joe's voice. The nice older man who'd sat at my table at The Black Swan—the place we'd stayed the night before our rafting trip. Then the other two must be Carlson, the pompous investor, and his previously subdued wife, Marlena.

I could tell that both Jonah and Brandi had figured out their identity, too. Their eyes were wide with recognition.

Mom had no clue who the people were. She was frantically trying to keep her balance in her crouched position.

"Why did you come out here with Astrid in the first place?" Carlson growled.

"I told you." Marlena's voice was like steel. "Astrid was worried the murder would be pinned on her. She'd dropped that stupid necklace of hers out here, and she didn't want the police to find it. I offered to help her look."

"But you hate Astrid," Carlson shot back. "Why would you come out here with her?"

"Really?" Marlena barked out a laugh. "How did you expect me to feel about her after your little fling?"

Uh oh. Carlson and Astrid did have an affair. I'd suspected something was going on with them when I'd seen them at the outdoor Shakespeare performance. But at that time, Astrid had seemed annoyed with Carlson. He'd been flirting with her, and she wasn't having any of it.

Mom's legs shook, and she grimaced. "My knees," she mouthed.

I put my hand on her arm to steady her.

"We need to get out of here before someone finds the body," Joe said.

Carlson grumbled something, and the three began walking toward the vehicles.

"We'll need to take Astrid's car and dump it somewhere," Marlena said. "It's got my DNA in it. Maybe we can set it on fire after we drive it to a different location."

"Do you have her keys?" Carlson asked.

"No," she answered angrily. "Why would I?"

"God, Marlena. You are dense. We'll need to retrieve the keys from her body so we can move her car."

"I'll get them," Joe said. His footsteps crunched toward the river. The footsteps came to a halt. "Guys… wasn't Astrid face down in the water when we left her?"

"Yeah, why?" Carlson said.

"She's face up now. Someone's been here."

CHAPTER 29

"Quick," Carlson said. "We need to find whoever turned Astrid over and get rid of them. They saw our vehicle—they probably even saw us."

Marlena's voice was tense. "I hope they weren't here when I shot her."

My stomach lurched. Why had Marlena killed Astrid?

I turned my head to look at Jonah, Brandi, and Mom. Their wide eyes and pale faces told me they were just as stunned as I was.

Mom wobbled in her squat and grimaced as she did her best to hold her position. I knew her knees were causing her pain. She wouldn't be able to stand it much longer.

"Where do we look?" Marlena said.

"Look for footprints or broken branches." Carlson crunched away. I heard him rooting through bushes and pushing branches aside. At least he wasn't near us anymore.

But the thought of them finding us made my blood pump wildly.

We had no weapons. All they had to do was shoot us and stuff us in Astrid's car before they set it on fire or pushed it over a cliff.

No. We had to take them by surprise if we wanted to get out of this alive. Or, we had to make it to our car and get the hell out of here before they could find us.

I had no idea how we could manage either option.

"Think, Clarity, think." I mulled the two ideas over. Which option was least likely to get us killed?

Joe and Carlson were big men. Though Jonah was tall, I didn't think he could fight off two men who each outweighed him by twenty pounds or more. Then there was Brandi, Mom, and me. I could use my newly acquired self-defense skills. But my skills were no match for Marlena's gun.

The arguing started up again, buying us some time.

"If you hadn't killed Arnold, none of this would be happening right now." Carlson's voice echoed off the trees.

"Look, I'm sorry," Joe said. "But he'd just told me he'd gambled all our money away. I mean, I lost fifty grand to that guy. That was part of my retirement money! My wife is gonna kill me when she finds out!"

"But you killed him," Marlena said. "He had our money, too. Now we'll never get it back."

"I smacked him with the oar in the heat of the moment," Joe grumbled. "I didn't intend to kill him. I was just mad."

Carlson snorted. "Arnold was going to own fifty percent of Ray's company once he gave that money to his dear cousin. And we would've had our names on the contract too. We'd be part owners in one of the most lucrative adventure travel companies in the country. Sure, he shouldn't have gambled it all away, but if he was alive, we might have been able to figure out a way to at least get some of the money back. Sell his car or something."

What? I thought Ray had just pulled a huge number off the top of his head, knowing that Arnold would never be able to raise the funds to become a partner. I guess Arnold had taken him seriously and decided to join up with some shady characters to get it done.

Marlena laughed, but it was a laugh that had zero merriment to it. "Joe, you lost your temper and killed a man. Now we're all on the hook for his murder."

"You're one to talk, Marlena," Joe said dryly. "You lost your temper and killed Astrid."

"No, I *planned* it. She had it coming. She slept with my husband. Plus, she was panicking. I found out she had an appointment to talk with those two detectives from Seattle. We all know how that would've ended. She would've told them everything."

The pieces were starting to come together.

"You didn't have to kill her," Carlson said under his breath.

"How did you get her to come out here?" Joe asked.

Marlena chuckled. "Easy. I told her I'd help her look for her stupid Olympics necklace. She was sure she'd dropped it near where Arnold was killed. After you hit Arnold in the back of the head with the paddle, you came to get us, and we all stood around his body trying to figure out what to do."

"And?" Joe asked.

"And she lost her necklace. But what she didn't know was that I found it on the day of Arnold's death and put it in my pocket. Astrid didn't like me, but she was desperate to get that necklace back. So, she was eager for help. But she was on the verge of cracking. It was only a matter of time before she told the police."

"Damn it. This is getting way too complicated. We just need to get the hell out of here before the cops come," Carlson muttered.

"But first we have to take out whoever found Astrid," Marlena said. "They may have seen something."

Oh, crap. We needed to get away. Now.

A rustling sound interrupted my thoughts. What was that?

Mom swayed precariously on the back of her heels. She grabbed onto a nearby rotting log to steady herself. The hollowed-out log rocked a bit, and then something emerged from one end.

Mom squinted at the creature with furrowed brows. "A kitten," she mouthed at me.

Confused, I tried to catch a glimpse of the animal, but all I saw was black fur.

Another little black thing toddled out of the end of the log.

"More kittens!" Mom said, but a little more loudly this time.

Terrified the bad guys might hear her, I aggressively put my finger to my lips. "Shhh!"

"What was that?" Marlena said?

"What?" Carlson said from a distance.

"I heard something!" Marlena came closer to our hiding place.

I glared at Mom. We were going to die all because of a family of cats!

Mom had already picked up one of the babies and was holding it in her palms. She stroked its soft fur.

Meanwhile, I began a panic attack. Marlena was going to find us! She had a gun! Mom was petting a kitten, talking to it in soothing tones.

Wait. Why were kittens living in a log in the middle of the woods?

Marlena's footsteps crunched past us as she tried to identify where the sound was coming from.

I leaned closer to Mom to warn her.

That's when the full extent of horror hit me. The kittens weren't cats. They were baby skunks. Mom didn't have her glasses on!

Frantically, I motioned for Mom to put the kitten down.

"What?" Mom said.

"Put it down!" I hissed. "It's a skunk!"

Mom furrowed her brows. "A what?" she said a little too loudly.

"Over here!" Marlena called to the guys. "I heard someone talking!"

"We'll be right there," one of the guys yelled.

It was too late. They'd found us. My eyes darted from Mom to the baby skunk. Without thinking, I snatched the little one from Mom's lap and threw it into a pile of soft leaves near Marlena.

The baby made chirping noises. It was in distress.

The log near Mom rocked again, and out came a much bigger skunk.

Oh, damn.

Mama skunk eyed me maliciously and trundled after her baby, tail raised, ready to spray.

I gasped.

Four more babies followed behind their mama, which was a blessing, because she clearly wasn't about to put her babies in the line of fire.

I heard Marlena hurrying toward us. "I hear them! They're close."

The skunk family scurried toward Marlena, but not fast enough. Knowing this was our only chance for a getaway, I stood and roared as loud as I could.

Marlena shrieked.

Mama skunk startled and ran forward—right into the path of Marlena and friends. Then she stopped and eyed the bad guys before turning her backside toward them, her tail sticking straight up.

I grabbed Mom's arm. "Come on! Run!" I took off, pushing Mom along as fast as we could go. "To the river!"

"My eyes!" screamed Marlena.

A cloud of putrid spray had reached its destination. I caught a whiff of it as it settled around the group of killers.

Behind us, the screams and howls filled the forest as mama skunk sprayed the bad guys with all she had.

CHAPTER 30

The howls and curses continued as we ran toward the river. I had a firm grip on Mom, so she wouldn't fall. We would never get away in time if she stumbled.

"Don't let them get away!" Marlena shrieked.

"God damn it!" Carlson yelled. "I can't see! My eyes are burning."

"Mine too," Joe thundered. "But we have to stop them!"

The men crashed through the brush, swearing as they ran.

"Come on!" I hissed.

We ran alongside the edge of the river, looking for something—anything to help us escape.

"There!" Jonah yelled. He pointed to a log perched on a rock. "Help me shove it into the water."

We bent over and pushed with all our might.

"They're over here!" one of the men hollered.

My heart pounded so loudly in my chest I could almost hear it over the roar of the river.

The log gave way and began to float. Pushing it further out, we each grabbed on with an arm slung over the top. I took a quick glance back.

Joe reached the river's edge. "There they are! Who's got the gun?"

Oh my God. They were going to shoot us! I looked over my shoulder as Carlson stumbled to Joe's side.

"I've got the gun, but I can't see a thing." He handed it to Joe.

"I can't either. Maybe if I just point in that direction, I'll hit one of them." Joe held the gun out.

The first shot hit the opposite bank well away from us.

"You idiot!" Carlson yanked the gun away from Joe. "Point it at the log."

We hit deeper water, and the river pulled our vessel faster downstream.

"Duck under water!" I screamed. I watched as they followed my orders, all but their arms disappearing under the swirling surface.

I held my breath and still holding onto the log, I plunged my head under the frigid water. A shot rang out. The bullet thumped into the log where my head would've been. I felt the vibration of it ripple through my body.

When I couldn't hold my breath any longer, I popped back up and filled my lungs with cool, clean air.

I chanced another look over my shoulder.

Emboldened by his near hit, Carlson had the gun pointed right at us. But he and Joe were much further away than they were the last time they shot.

"Duck under again!" I called.

We plunged back underneath the roiling river.

Finally, when my lungs felt they would burst, I resurfaced. Mom, Brandi, and Jonah, eyes wide, were panicked, waiting for me to come up.

"Thank God," Mom sputtered, looking like a wet chicken. "I thought they got you."

"No, I'm good."

I turned to look back at Joe and Carlson, but they weren't standing in the same spot anymore. They were stumbling alongside the river, trying to keep up with our log.

The pace of the river increased. I had no idea what was coming next. This was a part we hadn't gotten to on our rafting trip. Were there rapids ahead? Or a waterfall?

In any case, I was glad we were moving faster than Joe and Carlson could run.

"Should we try to make it to shore?" Brandi called from her spot in the front of the log.

"Not yet!" I yelled. "Joe and Carlson are still after us."

Mom looked tired. I was worried she was too cold to hold on to the log. "Hang on, Mom. It might get bumpy up ahead so hang on tight."

After we passed an outcrop of dense trees, the river opened wider and flowed at what seemed like a snail's pace.

Joe and Carlson were likely stuck back in the trees, trying to battle through the brush.

Could we get out here where the bank on the right was barely sloped or would that make us an easy target if the bad guys caught up to us?

The opposite bank of the river would be the obvious choice to make a getaway. The killers would have to swim across the river to get to us. I glanced at it as we floated along. It looked treacherous. The steep cliff wall would make it difficult for us to climb out. We'd have to get off on the right bank instead.

In the distance, sirens blared.

Had Brandi's call to Zen gotten through after all?

An ember of hope burned in my chest.

"Sirens!" Jonah yelled.

"Let's move to the shore!" I called, kicking my feet in frog paddles toward the bank of the river.

The current was strong, however we managed to pull through the water until our feet finally reached the bottom.

"You can let go of the log." Jonah gave it a push, and our trusty boat floated away.

I can't feel my legs." Mom moaned and struggled to walk against the current. Her face was pale in the afternoon sun.

I grabbed her arm. "Are you okay?" Jonah grabbed the other. We half-carried her to shore and set her gently down on the river's pebbled edge.

Brandi collapsed beside her. "It's okay. Let's rest a bit."

I rubbed Mom's blue legs to see if I could get her circulation going.

"Thanks, honey." She gave me a weary smile. "Pussy Galore is a tough old broad. She'll be fine in a few minutes."

I laughed. "I'm sure she will."

"Get out of my way!" a muffled voice yelled from the clump of trees we'd floated past. "You almost tripped me, you fool!"

Oh, crap. The killers were catching up. We didn't have time to let Mom rest. We had to run.

Mom scrambled to her feet, water dripping off her in rivulets. "Let's boogie. They're closing in."

"This way!" Jonah called. He dragged Brandi along, crashing through the knee-high grass on the upper bank.

Mom and I raced behind them into a small meadow. Crickets hopped out of the way as we blundered through the yellow grass. The sirens were loud now. We were almost safe.

"Not so fast." Marlena appeared from behind a tree, gun pointed straight at us.

We froze, not daring to breathe.

"I thought the men had the gun," Mom said.

Marlena's blinking gaze landed on Mom. Her eyes were still watering from the skunk spray, but she was otherwise calm and collected. "They're inept. I caught up to them stumbling through the trees and took it away. Like taking candy from a baby."

Suddenly, Joe and Carlson emerged from the forest behind Marlena, sweaty, stinky, and breathing hard.

"Marlena!" Carlson huffed and leaned forward, hands on his knees. "We've got to get out of here! Can't you hear the sirens?"

Without turning her head to address them, she said, "We can't let them live. They know who we are. Do you want to spend the rest of your life running from the police?"

Jesus. She was going to shoot us all.

Carlson and Joe approached nervously, glancing in the direction of the sirens.

"Come on, Marlena." Carlson's voice was soothing. "If we run now, we might be able to get away."

She shook her head. "No."

The sirens were loud, and in my estimation, were coming from where we'd parked Jonah's car. How much time would it take them to find us? Would they know we'd gone down river?

In the distance, the drone of a helicopter chopped through the air.

Marlena was crazy. Common sense and reason was not going to cut it. I had to distract her and buy us some time.

"Why did Astrid accept your offer to help her find her necklace?" I blurted out.

Her eyebrows rose. "Why do you care?"

I shrugged. "I mean, I thought she'd be wary of you considering she slept with your husband."

Marlena narrowed her eyes. "She was desperate. She didn't want the police to find the necklace and implicate her in Arnold's death." She waved the gun at the two men who'd come up beside her. "And neither of these idiots realized she was a liability."

Carlson and Joe exchanged an uneasy glance.

"I never liked Astrid," I offered, hoping to get Marlena even more riled up. "She was always trying to cozy up to men that weren't hers to take. Isn't that right, Brandi?"

Brandi frowned. "What? Oh, yeah. Astrid had a thing for Ray—but Ray wasn't interested in her. We had just starting dating..."

With their backs to the woods, the killers didn't notice the movement in the trees behind them.

Marlena snorted. "She was a conniving whore who thought she could have anything she wanted. Those Olympic medals she won? She earned those. But she didn't earn my husband. I'm the one who put up with his shady financial deals, his lack of motivation, and his infidelities." She spat out the last word as if it had left a bad taste in her mouth.

Carlson clenched his fists and shook his head. He took a step toward Marlena.

Hunter emerged from the trees a hundred feet away, his gun raised. "Police! Put your weapon down and your hands up!" he shouted.

Marlena whirled around, gun aimed at Hunter.

Without hesitation, I crouched low and flung myself at her legs, taking her down at the knees. The gun fired, the blast echoing off the cliffside on the opposite bank of the river.

Blood pounded in my ears. What had I done? Had she shot Hunter?

More shouts and rustling noises came from the woods as several police officers burst into the field, guns drawn.

Marlena squirmed underneath me as she tried to get away.

With a jolt of fear, I realized she still had a hold of her weapon. I watched as she wrenched her right arm free and tried to point the gun at me.

If she shot now, I'd be dead.

Wrestling her, I grabbed her gun hand. We rolled through the high grass as she tried to gain control.

Suddenly, a banshee shriek split the air above us. Something landed on me with its full weight, causing me to squash Marlena like a bug.

"Oof." Marlena let out a breath.

The shrieking creature on my back yanked the gun out of Marlena's hand, and rolled off me.

It was Mom.

"Freeze, bitch." Mom's voice was laced with menace.

Marlena screamed in frustration, but gave up the struggle and lay limp on the ground beneath me.

I clambered off the motionless woman and got to my knees, staring at Mom with wonder.

Mom, still looking like a wet chicken and reeking of skunk, pointed the gun straight at Marlena and growled, "Nobody messes with my daughter, and nobody messes with Pussy Galore."

CHAPTER 31

Zen came crashing out of the forest to stand beside Hunter. He looked frantically from me to Mom to Marlena. "Mom?"

Without taking her eyes off her prey, Mom said, "It's Pussy. Pussy Galore."

Zen winced. "Mom, drop your weapon."

He and Hunter slowly worked their way toward us through the low brush, guns trained on Marlena.

Behind them, more police officers emerged from the trees.

Zen turned to the officers behind him. "Arrest these two." He pointed at Joe and Carlson, who were attempting to slink back into the forest.

"Mom," Zen repeated. "Drop your weapon."

Mom frowned and lowered the gun.

Before I could react, Marlena scrambled to her feet and took off running toward the river.

"Damn it!" Mom shouted and went tearing after her.

"Mom, no!" I joined the chase.

Hunter and Zen were already in full pursuit and got to Mom first.

"I've got her." Zen grabbed Mom by the wrist and took the gun away. Pointing at Marlena, he shouted, "Get Marlena before she jumps in the river."

The helicopter was now hovering over the water, making giant ripples as it closed in on Marlena.

"Stop right there!" Hunter hollered over the thrum of the aircraft.

Marlena glanced at us over her shoulder before taking a giant, sprawling leap into the river.

"Damn it." Hunter growled and turned back to Zen.

"Let Marlena go," Zen said, still holding Mom by the arm. "The chopper will track her and then direct the sheriff's men to pick her up downstream."

The killer let out a loud yelp, her arms flailing as the current pulled her along. "Help! I can't swim!"

Mom rolled her eyes. "God. She's not only crazy, she's stupid too."

Brandi nodded. "Yeah. That was a dumb move."

"I'll get her." Jonah waded into the river. "I still have my lifeguard credentials."

Zen seemed unsure. "I don't think that's a good idea. We don't know what the water looks like up ahead. There could be rapids. No use putting your life in danger too. The officer in the helicopter will make the call if we need a rescue, okay?"

Jonah looked both disappointed and relieved. He waded back to shore. "Okay."

More sirens sounded in the distance.

Zen turned to Jonah. "Why don't you and Clarity go along the river's edge with Hunter. See if you can keep up with Marlena as she floats along. I'll stay here with my mom and Brandi." He glanced at Mom.

I knew he was concerned that Mom would want to come with us and possibly put herself in danger again.

Mom looked disappointed. "Brandi and I should help too."

Brandi, still soaking wet and looking totally trashed, stayed quiet.

"No. Hunter's got a gun. I'd rather you stay out of the line of fire," Zen said to Mom. "Come on. Let's make sure those two guys are cuffed and safely tucked into the back of the patrol cars."

Mom's eyes lit up. "Can I interrogate them?"

Zen groaned. "Nope. I think we've got that covered."

"Come on." Hunter laid his hand on my shoulder and pointed downriver. "Let's see if we can catch up to Marlena."

Jonah and I ran after Hunter as he jumped over logs and large rocks on the river's edge.

I caught sight of Marlena's head bobbing up and down in the water. "There she is!"

The helicopter whipped the air overhead, the wind drying my hair and clothing as I ran.

"Help!" gurgled Marlena. I could barely hear her over the noise of the helicopter.

Hunter's radio crackled. He slowed his run while he answered it. "Got it. We'll do our best."

I jogged alongside him. "Any news?"

"There's rapids ahead. She's heading straight toward them."

"Oh, no." Jonah rushed ahead of Hunter. "I should've gone in after her."

"No," Hunter said. "Zen's right. You shouldn't endanger your life. Then we'd be rescuing two people, not one."

"Do you think we can get her out before she hits them?" I panted. A stitch in my side was making it painful to run.

"I sure as hell hope so." Hunter picked up his pace, catching up to Jonah.

I swore. "I should've kept up my gym membership."

Hunter slowed and looked over his shoulder. "Are you okay? Take a breather and sit on that log." He pointed to an overturned tree higher up on the riverbank.

He didn't know I had a stubborn streak a mile wide. "No, I've got this," I said, not really believing it.

A hundred yards ahead, Marlena bobbed up and down in the fast-moving water. Her arms flailed as she tried to keep her head above the current. She was approaching boulders the size of small cars. Logs and other debris were trapped on the edges. White water rushed in between the obstacles.

"Almost there!" Hunter shouted.

I watched the guys sprint away. I couldn't keep up. The stitch in my side was growing more painful with each breath.

Finally allowing myself to slow down, I took in a shallow breath. Even as I watched Hunter and Jonah get level with Marlena struggling in the water, I knew there was no way they could pull her out.

The helicopter chopping above moved into position directly over the drowning woman. Could they rescue her?

I stopped and peered up at the aircraft.

Hunter yelled something over the noise. I couldn't quite catch what he was saying.

Marlena had reached the rocks.

The water greedily sucked her through an opening, and she disappeared from view.

I ran on, ignoring the pain in my side. "Jonah! Hunter! Where did she go?" I couldn't see past the big rocks and had no idea what was on the other side.

Hunter shook his head.

"Doesn't look good!" Jonah shouted.

To my right was an access road. Dust rose up into the hot summer air as police cars, fire trucks, and ambulances screeched to a halt where the road ended. Police officers hurried to join Hunter and Jonah, talking into their radios and strategizing their next moves.

Precious seconds dragged into too many minutes.

Medical personnel from the first ambulance to arrive poured out of the vehicle and dashed alongside the river, heading toward the place where Marlena was last seen.

Jonah followed them. "I'm going to see if they need any help getting her out of the water."

I approached Hunter cautiously, not wanting to startle the officers.

"Clarity." Hunter pulled me to his side. "What the hell is going on with this woman? I caught part of Brandi's message about Astrid being killed. Can you fill me in?"

"It's complicated," I told him. "In a nutshell, Joe killed Arnold because he found out that Arnold had gambled away the money they were going to invest in Ray's business. Then they tried to cover up the murder. Astrid slept with Marlena's husband and she was about to tell the police who had killed Arnold.

Marlena tricked Astrid into letting her help her find the necklace Astrid dropped at the crime scene. Then Marlena shot her."

Hunter raised one eyebrow. "What?"

I shrugged. "I'll give you more details later when you write your report."

"But what about Dr. Strong?" Hunter asked.

"Oh, I don't think he had anything to do with either murder. He's just a scumbag."

"He wasn't involved in any of this?"

"Not really. But you should interview him just in case. He thinks we have a date at six o'clock, remember?" I slapped at a mosquito buzzing near my ear. "Though I don't ever want to see him again."

"Don't worry. Zen and I will take care of interviewing him," Hunter said. "What is his connection to Arnold? Do you know?"

"Nathan wanted to buy into Ray's business too. He gave Arnold some money, but just found out that Arnold gambled it away. He's pretty pissed, but I don't think he had a part in the murders."

"Gotcha," Hunter said. His radio crackled.

The garbled sound of speech came through it. I didn't understand a thing, but Hunter must have.

"They found Marlena floating below the rapids. She's dead."

CHAPTER 32

I watched as the medics carried Marlena's lifeless body toward the open ambulance doors. Her skin had a bluish tinge to it, and her head seemed to be cocked at an unnatural angle.

"Broken neck," Hunter said grimly.

"Damn." Jonah sighed. "She was a terrible person, but I didn't want her to die."

"Yeah." I felt a twinge of sadness as the ambulance doors slammed shut. "She was so hellbent on not being arrested. I guess she was willing to take the risk of dying rather than being locked up."

Hunter put his arm around my shoulder. "Come on. Let's go back to where our vehicles are. I want to check in with Zen and let him know what happened."

The walk back along the river and then through the forest took longer than I expected. By the time we made it back to where the skunk incident happened, I felt like I would drop from exhaustion.

Jonah and Hunter had been relatively quiet the whole way back, and I definitely hadn't felt like talking either.

Once we got to the spot where Zen's car and a few other police vehicles were haphazardly parked, I heard raised voices. I watched an ambulance roll away toward the main road.

"They must have collected Astrid's body," I whispered as we approached the police cars.

"No doubt." Hunter stopped for a moment to observe the argument between Zen and the other policemen.

Zen, Brandi, and Mom were standing next to three officers. Two of the officers were attempting to put Joe and Carlson in Zen's car.

I wrinkled my nose. The stench wafting off the two captives was vomit-inducing.

"Absolutely not!" Zen shouted. "I don't want this car smelling like a skunk. Put 'em in your patrol car."

Mom was grinning from ear to ear, clearly amused and delighted to be a witness to it all. "You could always strap them to a log and float them downriver. Maybe the water would wash off some of their stink."

Joe gave her an alarmed look. "No! You can't do that. That's police brutality!"

Zen glared at Mom. "I know you're not serious, so let's not upset the prisoners, okay?"

She shrugged. "I'm half serious. Do you want them to stink up your car?"

"I don't," Zen growled. "That's why they should be put in a patrol car."

One of the officers sighed. "All right. Put 'em in mine. I have a couple of days off. Maybe I can get my car de-skunked by the time I go back to work."

"Thank you, Glenn," Zen said. "That was big of you."

The officer shrugged. "You owe me, though."

"Fine." Zen watched Joe and Carlson climb into the back seat of a patrol car. "I'll buy you a beer."

"Make that two." The officer got in the driver's seat and rolled down all the windows. "I don't get paid enough for stuff like this."

Hunter chuckled. "You guys have been arguing about this the entire time we were chasing Marlena?"

Brandi nodded. "Pretty much. They've been at it for a while now."

"It was like watching a tennis match between Billie Jean King and Bobby Riggs! The back and forth was super entertaining." Mom laughed.

I didn't know who either of those people were, but it didn't matter. Mom was still in good humor, considering she was wet and bedraggled.

"What happened to Marlena?" Zen asked. "Did you get her?"

Hunter frowned. "Yeah. But she didn't make it. The rapids pulled her through some big rocks. and she broke her neck."

Mom stared at him. "She… died?"

I stepped closer to her and squeezed her arm, wondering if she felt like it was her fault somehow. "Marlena decided to take that risk when she jumped in the water. She could've given herself up."

"Dang." Mom looked down at her feet. "I feel kind of bad."

"You shouldn't. It wasn't your fault," Brandi said. "Like Clarity said, Marlena made some pretty bad choices."

"Yeah," Jonah offered. "Once she killed Astrid, every decision she made was a bad one."

"Her first bad decision was marrying Carlson," Brandi said.

Mom sniffed. "I guess so." She glanced back at Jonah's car further up the gravel road. "Can we get back to the farm now? I think it's time Pussy Galore got back to tending the goats."

***

Dad was just coming out of the barn when we pulled up the driveway. He took one look at us and raised his eyebrows. "What in the world happened to you?"

"Don't ask." Mom's shoulders slumped.

"Wanda? Are you all right?" Dad rushed forward and put his arm around her waist. "How did this happen?"

"Well," Mom grumbled. "If you must know, we found the supermodel chick dead in the water. She'd been shot. And then the bad guys came back, and they were going to kill us too, but we used a skunk on them. They had a gun and they chased us to the river, so we had to grab a log and jump in. The bad guys kept shooting at us, and then the crazy lady got the gun from the other two dudes, and she was gonna kill us. But Clarity tackled her, and they fought, so I had to get in the mix, and I got the gun away from the crazy lady. That's when Zen and Hunter showed up, and then the crazy lady jumped into the river. But the fool couldn't swim, so she got sucked down the rapids, and she died."

Dad gave her a funny look. "Have you been smokin' weed? I thought you gave that up."

Mom frowned at him. "No! Haven't you been listening?"

I stifled a giggle. "We'll fill you in later, Dad. Mom needs to take a nice hot bath and relax a little. She's had a rough day."

"No." Mom winced. "No more soaks in water. A quick shower will do."

Dad scratched his head. "If you say so." He looked the rest of us up and down. "Looks like you could all use a shower. I'm going back to muck out the barn."

Mom opened the door to the house. The two puppies, Comet and Kodiak, came out to greet us, tails wagging exuberantly.

"Puppies!" Brandi shouted and picked one of them up and stroked its soft fur. "With all the craziness going on at the river, I'd completely forgotten about them."

"Puppies make everything better," Jonah said, picking the other little dog up.

Pumpkin appeared in the doorway with Jolie, the goat. My orange tabby sauntered over to me and rubbed his cheek on my leg, purring.

"Have you and Jolie been babysitting the puppies while we were gone?" I asked him.

As if in answer, Pumpkin let out a loud meow.

I laughed and scratched under his chin. "You're a good nanny. I hope you'll still like Kodiak when we take him home to Seattle."

"Is Hunter taking Comet home or is he riding with us?" Jonah asked.

I shrugged. "I don't know. We haven't discussed that yet. I'm assuming he'll take him since Comet is his dog."

"You guys better stay together as a couple," Brandi said. "Those pups would be sad if they didn't get to see each other."

I froze. I hadn't thought about that. In fact, I hadn't had time to think about much else since Arnold had been murdered.

"Brandi—speaking of staying together, now that we know who killed Arnold, Ray should be getting out of jail soon! Has he texted you yet?"

"Oh my God! You're right!" She patted her pocket for her phone, and her face fell. "It's gone. It must've fallen out in the river."

Jonah and I suddenly reached for our phones as well. We each pulled ours out of our wet pockets and frowned.

"Dead." I tried in vain to get it to come back to life.

"Mine too." Jonah used the bottom of his damp shirt to wipe off the screen. "Damn. I just bought this one. Water damage isn't covered in the warranty."

"Why don't you go ask my Dad if you can use his flip phone," I told Brandi.

She pooched out her lip. "I can't. I don't know Ray's number. It was in my address book… On my phone."

"That sucks. We'll have to wait until we can talk to Zen and Hunter. They probably won't be back until they've written up their reports and dealt with the prisoners." Just as the last words were out of my mouth, I heard a car engine approaching.

We stood and stared as dust billowed around the vehicle. It came to a stop in front of us.

Zen and Hunter's car was barely recognizable covered in layers of dirt and dust.

Before I could react, the back door opened, and Ray climbed out. He stepped into the sunshine, wearing the same suit he had on when he was arrested after Arnold's funeral.

"Ray!" Brandi practically threw the puppy she was holding at me and went to hug her boyfriend. She cupped his face with her hands. "Oh, my God! Is it really you? Are you okay? I missed you!"

Ray wrapped his arms around Brandi and smiled. "It's really me. I missed you too." He kissed her and then stepped back and looked at all of us. "Zen and Hunter told me what you did to prove that I didn't kill Arnold. I can't thank you enough."

"We couldn't let an innocent man be punished for something he didn't do," I said.

"Well, I honestly don't know how to repay you." Ray grinned.

"You can start by taking me out to dinner when we get back to Seattle." Brandi giggled.

"Just name the restaurant, and I'll take you there." He put his arm around her.

Zen and Hunter got out of the dirt-mobile and joined our little circle.

Jonah handed Hunter the red puppy.

Hunter smiled and kissed the puppy's head. "Thanks. Looks like you guys are taking good care of Comet for me."

"He's been looked after by Pumpkin and Jolie," I said.

"Too bad we can't take Jolie home with us, too." He winked at me. "Hey, would you mind watching my pup for another few hours? Zen and I are heading back to the station to wrap up the case."

"No problem. We're not going anywhere tonight." I put Kodiak down and watched him plunk down next to Pumpkin. "Will you be back for dinner?"

"Sure. We should be back around seven-thirty." Hunter kissed my cheek.

Zen eyed us suspiciously but then seemed to remember we were officially a couple. "Want us to bring anything for tonight?"

"Wine!" Brandi and I said simultaneously.

"Beer," Jonah added.

Zen laughed. "How about you, Ray?"

Ray shrugged. "I don't care. I'll drink anything."

"Okay, we'll bring a variety." The detectives got in the car and turned it around, heading back out the long dirt road.

✳✳✳

Mom turned on the garden lights, even though the sun was still painting the sky in tangerine hues. The patio Dad had built seemed magical, nearly twinkling with wisteria-draped arches. Bright orange honeysuckle plants were rooted in large ceramic pots at each corner.

A large dairy cow wandered through the yard—the same one that we'd nearly hit with the truck while we'd been tailing Astrid on the way to the casino. Mom had sent Dad out to rescue her while we made dinner.

Ray had changed out of his suit and into some of Dad's clothes, which made him look less funereal and more like a hippie. The worn jeans and tie-dye t-shirt hung loosely on him.

For the past couple of hours, we'd all worked together in the kitchen to make fried chicken, potato salad, and a fruit plate.

"Ah, here they are." Dad pointed at the vehicle driving toward the house. "Just in time."

The car stopped. Zen got out and opened one of the back doors. He took out a couple of grocery bags. "Booze, anyone?"

"I'll help you with that, son." Dad jumped up and took one of the bags. Hunter joined them, carrying a bottle of whiskey.

They disappeared into the kitchen and came back a few minutes later carrying glasses and opened bottles.

Hunter took a seat next to me and gave me a warm smile, his eyes sparkling in the twinkling garden lights.

The cat, puppies, and little goat were all conked out in the grass nearby.

We filled our glasses and raised them in the dwindling sunset.

"To solving murders!" Jonah said.

"To Ray's freedom," Brandi added.

"To Pussy Galore!" I clinked Mom's glass with my own.

"To relationships old and new." Hunter clinked his glass with Mom and Dad's, then Brandi's and Ray's, and then mine.

A strange feeling came over me—one that I'd always wished for but hadn't quite managed to achieve until now. It was a feeling of genuine belonging.

ABOUT THE AUTHOR

Martina Dalton writes young adult fiction and lives in the Pacific Northwest with her family. Born and raised in Alaska, she can nimbly catch a fish, dress for rain, and know what to do when encountering a grizzly bear. Now living in the Seattle area, she uses those same skills to navigate through rush-hour traffic.

If you liked this book, please consider leaving a review!

Visit the website at www.martinadalton.com to join my mailing list and get the latest news on upcoming books, giveaways, and more!

I love connecting with readers. Follow me on Instagram **@martinadaltonauthor** or Facebook **@AuthorMartinaDalton**!

Other books by Martina Dalton
Killer Bait: A Clarity Bloom Humorous Mystery Novel
The Third Eye of Jenny Crumb
The Sixth Sense of Jenny Crumb
The Nine Lives of Jenny Crumb
The Witching Hour: Jenny Crumb
Night Collector: Jenny Crumb
Jenny Crumb and the Twelve Days of Christmas (novella)

If you liked Killer Rapids, stay tuned for the next books in the series coming soon!

ACKNOWLEDGMENTS

I'd like to give special thanks to my writing critique partners, Brenda Beem, Dennis Robertson, Fabio Bueno, Suma Subramaniam, Maren Higbee, and Eileen Riccio. I'd also like to thank my editor, Alyssa Palmer.

Thanks for reading! Please consider leaving a review on Amazon and let me know what you thought!

Visit the website at **www.martinadalton.com** to join my mailing list and get the latest news on upcoming books, giveaways, and more!